# Eleanor's Secret REVEALED

## BRENDA W. CRADDOCK

Typeset in Minion Pro

Editing, typesetting and publishing by UK Book Publishing

www.ukbookpublishing.com

ISBN: 978-1-914195-76-1

# Author's Note

Newcastle is the town of my birth and growing to adulthood. I love the town, though I now live in County Durham with my husband, a retired Consultant Anaesthetist. He is a great support as are our two daughters, Philippa, and Stephanie who has once again designed the cover of the book. Our grandchildren Annabel and Adam are always interested and encouraging.

# Eleanor's Secret
# *REVEALED*

# Chapter 1

The weeks following her mother's death were difficult for Eleanor. It had come as a great shock to receive the news that her mother had died, while Eleanor was on her honeymoon in 1898, and it was fortunate that Tom was such an understanding man because she was not the best of company and could hardly wait to get home again. Their honeymoon came to a very abrupt end. There was also the underlying situation of deceit and untruths to contend with and these were always on Eleanor's mind. Her father was dealing with Muriel's death better than she had expected which was a great relief. He believed that his wife's death was from natural causes and he did not question that at all. He never queried what had caused her mother to have such a severe asthma attack. She had not had a serious asthma attack since her early twenties and even then, it was nothing like as severe. There must have been a reason for the suddenness and severity of the attack, but Cyril did not question it, saying that it was just one of those extraordinary things which can occur. He had a very philosophic view on life and believed that 'in the midst of life we are in death' and we do not have ultimate control of our own lives.

Cyril felt himself very blessed that he had four sons and a daughter who gave him solace in his grief. They were all fine young people and he continued to be very proud of them. James being a doctor kept a caring eye on his father's health; Frank was an optimist, with a very cheerful disposition and being a railway engineer, always had something interesting to tell him about railways. Frank was very involved with the 'Railway Age' which had revolutionised travel in the 19th century. Harry visited his father often from the Naval College which he attended in North Shields and sometimes took him down to Whitley Bay and Tynemouth for a walk right along the seafront which he loved. Gone were the days when Harry had not been able to keep pace with his father. Now it was Harry in the lead and his father who had difficulty keeping up with his son, but this did not diminish his love of walking. The sea air was always very invigorating and lifted his spirits every time.

Perhaps most importantly Cyril did not live alone. His youngest son Benjamin was still living with him and Benjamin's girlfriend Victoria was a frequent visitor. He could see that they were very fond of one another and was not too surprised when Benjamin confided in him about six months after his mother's death, that he intended asking Victoria to marry him. Cyril could only express delight at this news. Benjamin had always been a quiet, reserved young man and Victoria was so good for him, being much more outgoing and vivacious. She and Eleanor, Benjamin's sister, had liked one another immediately and had become good friends. Victoria, like Eleanor, was able to empathise with Benjamin and encourage him to be at ease with people. Cyril certainly felt he understood Benjamin better now and was much more appreciative of his artistic gifts. The picture which Benjamin's mother had commissioned him to paint many years ago of the River Tyne, with its many sailing vessels, still hung on the wall in the 'drawing room' in their home at Summerhill. Eleanor also had a similar painting in her house which Tom had commissioned Benjamin to paint for him. The River Tyne had always been a favourite in the Delaney household. It had played an enormous part in Newcastle's origins and subsequent prosperity. It had great significance for Eleanor because it was beside the River Tyne that she had first met Tom, her beloved husband.

Victoria was also an artist, and she and Benjamin had met at an art club which was held in the large triangular shaped building in the centre of the town, very near Grey's Monument. It was generally called the Central Exchange and had been built between 1834 and 1838. It had several uses, principally as a newsroom but this was replaced by an Art Gallery, a Concert Hall and a Music Hall Theatre. The Art Club where Benjamin and Victoria met was housed in the Art Gallery within the Central Arcade.

The house in which Cyril and Benjamin lived in Summerhill, had a number of rooms which were not used now that his three elder sons and his daughter had left home and much to the delight of Benjamin and Victoria, Cyril had designated a room to them which they could use for their art and craft work, and the couple spent many happy hours there. They were very well suited, and Cyril was so relieved and happy that Benjamin had found such a nice young lady and was not taking himself so seriously. He was so much more relaxed and confident.

Cyril was a sensible man and knew that it was no good sitting feeling sorry for himself after Muriel died. He was approaching sixty years of age and would be retiring soon, and he was determined to get on with life and keep busy and be as useful as he could be to his family and friends. One of the ways he did this was to help Harry's friend Phillip and his wife Ella with their adopted daughter Annabel. He had really taken to that little girl when he met her at Tom and Eleanor's wedding. Both of her parents worked and needed someone to meet Annabel after school, even though she was now in the Junior School. They were very protective of her and needed to know that she got home safely every night. Cyril stepped up to this daily duty because he was always home by four o'clock and he loved meeting her from school. Annabel reminded him so much of Muriel with her tight blond golden curls and big blue eyes. She was a great chatterbox and the conversation between them was always interesting and lively. He looked forward to meeting Annabel every day from school and delivering her safely home after giving her something to eat. Her favourite thing was banana on toast and a lovely ginger biscuit with a drink of orange juice. He was reminded of the delicious ginger biscuits that Muriel used to make but Annabel did not seem to mind the bought ones he gave her. The partaking of tea was always interspersed with highlights of her school day. She had a lovely placid nature and an innate gentleness and kindness which reminded him so much of his beloved only daughter Eleanor.

In the aftermath of Muriel's death Eleanor did not have much time to think about the circumstances of it because she and Tom were kept busy making the house that they had bought in the Summerhill area, into a home. She was also always busy at school and often brought school-work home with her. Typically for her and other teachers, school did not end when the bell or buzzer indicated the end of the school day. but she loved her work and was very conscientious, as was Tom, and they always made time at weekends to do something or go somewhere together. They were still very good friends with Phillip and Ella and frequently went out with them on a Saturday evening. Cyril was a very willing babysitter for Annabel. Over time, Eleanor, Tom and Cyril considered them part of their family. In later years this was to be very significant. Eleanor was very glad to have a friend like Ella, being the only girl in her own family. She loved all four of her brothers dearly but there were things which you could not discuss with brothers, that you could with girlfriends.

Tom and Eleanor had been married about six months when Eleanor began feeling very tired and sickly in the morning. Her doctor confirmed what she had suspected. She was pregnant. She and Tom were delighted with the news. Almost at the same time Benjamin told the family that he had proposed to Victoria and they were getting married the following year, in 1899. That would be another special family occasion in 1899 and Cyril felt very blessed that he had so much to which he could look forward.

# Chapter 2

T hen came the day which changed everything. He and
Annabel were walking home from school, and she was
talking excitedly about Auntie Eleanor's baby, and suddenly
she said, 'Grandpa, what is a workhouse?'

'Why do you want to know that Annabel?' Cyril said.

'Someone at school said I was found on the step of a
workhouse, very early one morning.'

'How silly,' Cyril said, 'whoever told you that?'

'One of the children whose mother is a cleaner at our
school. She said it was in a newspaper about eight years ago,
about the time I was born, that a baby had been found on the
workhouse step and her mother has told her that because the
baby was adopted, I could be that baby.'

Cyril was puzzled and concerned. What had prompted
someone to say such a thing, he wondered.

'What nonsense,' he said now. 'Do not take any notice.
They are obviously talking about someone else.'

Fortunately, Annabel accepted this and said no more about it, but Cyril could not help feeling a little worried. He remembered that news item about a baby being found on the step of the workhouse. It was near that time when his wife had gone away to see her sister in Carlisle and had returned very early one morning, but she certainly did not have a baby with her. She had never really given a satisfactory explanation about returning so soon from her sister's and at such a ridiculous hour in the morning. Then Cyril dismissed these thoughts as being very fanciful. They refused to disappear, however, and the next time he saw Eleanor he could not resist telling her what Annabel had told him. He did not notice how alert Eleanor became to what he was saying. His words brought the past back in an instant. She would have to find out the name of this person who had prompted Annabel's question about workhouses. It was such a bad time to hear about this because it brought back memories of her mother and she had to admit that she was missing her mother very much in her pregnant state. It would have been wonderful to share the experience of carrying a child within her, with her very own mother, whom she was sure would have had some excellent advice to give her and would be able to fully empathise with her pregnancy. The latter was a time when daughters and mothers could be very close. Eleanor was very fortunate in that Tom's mother was very caring of her and of course was extremely excited about her first grandchild. She had got out her knitting needles almost immediately.

In the weeks that followed there was no recurrence of the name calling so Eleanor decided not to take any action. Surely after all this time the secret which she had kept about her mother for eight long years was not now going to come to light. The consequences would not be good for anyone, and she did not want anything to spoil the anticipation and birth of her first child.

Tom sensed that there was something bothering his wife, but she assured him she was fine, and it was the pregnancy that was making her moody and irritable at times. She could not help wondering if the time had come to share her secret with Tom. It would be such a relief to tell him so that they could talk freely about it. They were able to talk about anything and everything except her secret, which she was too afraid to share with anyone, even her lovely husband Tom. He was so excited at the thought that he was to become a father, although he recognised that it was a big responsibility and had to admit it was a little daunting.

Together Tom and Eleanor prepared a nursery for their baby. Tom had never painted before, but he painted the walls of the nursery and even made a beautiful crib for the new baby. He surprised himself with the new skills he was acquiring. Eleanor too was discovering things she could now do. She made curtains and beautiful drapes for the baby's crib. She remembered how good her mother was at sewing. She had made Eleanor's wedding dress with material bought at Bainbridge's Department Store in Newcastle, and that was where Eleanor went to buy material for the nursery curtains and the crib. She had to walk through the Bigg Market to get there and it was still the very busy thoroughfare that she remembered it being, when she and her mother shopped for material. She and Tom bought items of old furniture which Tom restored and painted, and Benjamin decorated the walls with his paintings of baby animals. The nursery looked beautiful, and Tom and Eleanor were very proud of their efforts. It made them more than ever excited about their new baby. Meanwhile Tom's mother Edith, Ella and Victoria, were busy knitting delightful baby garments and Annabel proudly presented a pair of bootees which her mummy had helped her to knit. Happiness and love were found in abundance in Tom and Eleanor's home, and nothing must be allowed to spoil it. Hopefully Annabel would not be bothered again by those nasty taunts.

Eleanor was not to know that her father was giving quite a lot of thought to Annabel's question about workhouses. Something disturbed him but he was not sure what it was. A workhouse, which was later modified to become one of Newcastle's leading hospitals, Newcastle General Hospital, had opened on the West Road in 1841 which was not too far away from Summerhill where they lived, and Cyril decided that he would visit it one day. He was true to his word and one day walked up the West Road to go there. He was invited into the building where he met the manager and his wife. He knew he would have to give a reason for his visit and found it necessary to tell a little white lie for which he hoped to be forgiven. It was not something he was in the habit of doing and he could not help feeling a little guilty. He told them that he was writing an article for a newspaper. Newcastle had two main newspapers at the time. The Gazette which was first produced in 1710 and the Newcastle Courant which was the first newspaper published in the North of England. Cyril had a newspaper brought to his house every morning, which he enjoyed reading while having his breakfast.

Cyril explained that he had been given the task of finding out more about workhouses for the newspaper for whom he worked because there was renewed interest in babies being abandoned at workhouses, such was the poverty in various parts of the city. The manager was happy to talk about it but said that it was not something that happened too often. One or two of the incidences were notable, however, and he went on to tell Cyril about such an incident a few years previously. It would always be remembered because the baby was very young, perhaps only a few days old, and had obviously been very well looked after as she was dressed in clean clothing and was well nourished. She was wrapped up warmly in a beautiful hand knitted shawl. All the signs of her being loved and looked after were there and her presence in the workhouse was a mystery. She was a beautiful baby and everyone who worked there had hoped that someone would come forward and claim her, but no-one ever did. They were, however, later told that she had been adopted.

Cyril went on to explain that he wanted his article to draw people's attention to young mothers who had no means of supporting their new-born babies and had no alternative but to abandon them in a place where they were sure to be found and looked after. He wanted to make an important point that these babies were denied a mother's love and attention, and this should not be allowed to happen.

Cyril was given a tour of the workhouse, but it only served to strengthen his belief that workhouses while providing shelter for the poor and needy in society, were not pleasant places in which to live. He thanked the manager for the information he had been given and it gave him food for thought as he walked home down the West Road. The story of the young, well cared for baby who was abandoned had touched his heart, but there was nothing at all to connect it with himself or his family. He knew Annabel was adopted but Ella and Phillip had never ever referred to a workhouse. He dismissed any thought of a connection from his mind, but there was still the question of why Annabel was being called names, which suggested she had something to do with a workhouse. He did not feel it appropriate to ask Ella and Phillip about Annabel's adoption and decided to let the matter rest for the time being and hope there were no more nasty taunts.

# Chapter 3

S everal weeks later Annabel was crying when she came out of school. Cyril was so used to her giving him a lovely smile as she skipped towards him that he was immediately concerned.

'Whatever is the matter, Annabel?' he said.

'Oh Grandpa, everyone is being horrible to me because they say I am a workhouse kid, dirty and smelly, but I am not, Grandpa, am I. Tell me I am not.'

'You are definitely not a workhouse child, Annabel and I am going to find out who is telling such nasty tales about you. We will dry your tears away and I will make you a special tea to make you feel better. How about at least two ginger biscuits?'

Grandpa Cyril was a hero in Annabel's eyes, and she knew he would sort it out for her. She did not need to worry, and Mummy did not need to know because it would only worry her, and her mummy worried about everything.

Cyril felt sure that the baby left on the workhouse step all those years ago could not have been Annabel. It was ridiculous to think such a thing, but it was still a mystery why the word workhouse was being used to taunt her. She did not even know what a workhouse was. The word workhouse, however, was very significant for Eleanor. She would never forget that fateful morning when she had gone out with Benjamin, her brother, to the Town Moor, very early in the morning so that he could paint the sunrise over the moor. He had to work quickly to catch the moment and it was almost daylight when they set off for home down Westgate Road to Summerhill. They had to pass the workhouse and it was at that point when Benjamin said he would hurry on and jog down Westgate Road because it would be good exercise for him. Recently he had noticed that he was putting on weight. It was when Eleanor was passing the workhouse that she saw a woman placing what looked like a big bundle of wool on the doorstep of the workhouse. She may have continued to think that until she heard in the silence of the early morning a baby's cry and realised that it was a baby being left there. As the woman turned away Eleanor wanted to shout out and move forward to stop her from leaving until she realised with horror that the woman was in fact her own mother. The shock and horror of the moment had rendered her immobile and speechless and by the time she recovered, her mother was out of sight, having run away as fast as she could down the West Road.

The most dreadful thing was that her mother never owned up to what she had done, and her father and brothers were completely ignorant of the fact that another baby had been born into their family, a sister for Eleanor and her brothers. Eleanor had been sure that her mother would open up about the baby, but she never did, and Eleanor was never able to speak about it because she felt strongly that the initiative should have come from her mother. It meant that Eleanor could never divulge what she had seen to anyone, and she had to continue to keep the secret of her mother's wrongdoing to herself. Over the years there were times when she was tempted to confide in Tom or her father and brothers, but decided against it every time, as it could greatly upset them. They may not even have believed her because it was a preposterous story.

Her brothers would probably deal with it better, although even they would be disgusted that their mother had abandoned her own baby. It had not been easy to keep the secret especially when it became obvious to her that Annabel was indeed her own sister and her father's child, and could even have been the reason for her mother's fatal asthma attack. Muriel had acted very strangely at the wedding meal by completely ignoring Annabel, the youngest bridesmaid. She must have realised at the wedding that Annabel, looking so like herself with the ash blonde very curly hair and big blue eyes could perhaps be the baby she had so cruelly abandoned nine years ago. It was even more believable when Annabel sang a solo at the wedding. She had a beautiful singing voice just like herself. It must have been a tremendous shock for her to be in the presence of her own child whom she had been desperate to keep secret. Eleanor had noticed her father and mother leaving the wedding celebrations quite early in the evening. No doubt Muriel could not run the risk of talking to Annabel and getting too emotional about it. Eleanor was so glad that no-one had seen her mother leaving the baby. That must remain a secret.

# Chapter 4

W hat Eleanor did not know, however, was that she was not the only person to see Muriel leave her baby at the workhouse that morning. Muriel had been so careful and so sure that no-one had seen her, but a member of staff was coming to work that morning very early, much sooner than she normally did and she recognised the woman who was leaving her baby on the workhouse step. There was no mistake because she had spent time in the past looking at her with hate in her heart. It was unbelievable. That woman was married to a man called Cyril. He probably would not know her, but she knew him, because he had worked at the same pottery as herself in the Ouseburn Valley, the Ouseburn being a tributary of the River Tyne. A variety of industries had premises in the valley including 'The Maling Pottery' which was reputed to be the best of its kind. Cyril and Doris had both started work there on leaving school. He was tall and very good looking, and Doris had admired him from afar. She even dreamt about him and engineered times when she would meet him in the street or factory. He took no notice of her, but in time she believed that she was passionately in love with him. She thought about him all the time. If she met him or passed him in the factory her cheeks flushed, and she had butterflies in her tummy, but she never plucked up enough courage to talk to him. Giving him a smile was as far as she got, but he never responded in any way. She was devastated when he left the factory and moved back to the area where he had been born, near the River Tyne in a place called Sandhill and she never expected to see him again, but sometime after Cyril left, her father got a new job in Lord Armstrong's shipyard on the River Tyne and the family moved to Sandhill. Knowing this was where Cyril had gone to live, she could hardly believe her luck and saw it as an opportunity to get to know Cyril better. She dreamt of making herself known to him and they would get into conversation and she would flatter him by telling him how handsome he was, and she convinced herself that he would be interested in her and even ask her out and be her boyfriend.

It was therefore quite a disappointment when she encountered Cyril in Sandhill one day, hand in hand with a young lady. She made enquiries about her and found out that her name was Muriel, who she had to admit was nice looking and had lovely thick very blonde and very curly hair It was quite distinctive really and she was close enough one day to see that she had the most beautiful big blue eyes. When she found out that they were married and even expecting their first child, her dream of becoming Cyril's wife was shattered.

Doris had no choice but to just get on with her life. She married, had three children and moved to the Elswick area of Newcastle. When her three children were old enough and more independent, she got a job at the new Workhouse on the West Road. The wage was not good, but it meant she could help to support her family's income. In fact, she was the breadwinner of the family. Her husband was so lazy, and she had lost count of the names she had called him in anger because of his laid-back attitude. She was the one going out to work and he ought to have been ashamed of himself, but of course nothing could shame him.

Thoughts of Cyril and his wife had been forgotten until the morning when she had to be at work much sooner than usual. It was very early in the morning and as she neared the workhouse, she saw a woman putting a baby on the front doorstep. She was just about to shout out when the woman turned to leave and she realised with a sense of shock that it was the woman Cyril had married, none other than her old heartthrob's wife. Whatever was she doing? Here was a nice bit of gossip. Doris loved gossip. She would have to tell the workhouse staff all about it, but then she decided not to say anything until she had had time to think more about it. Doris had no scruples. She knew Cyril and Muriel had money because her enquiries had shown her that he had a very good job and lived in Summerhill, which was a very good area. There could be money in this if she was to keep what she had seen a secret. There were bound to be queries when the baby was found on the doorstep, but she would say nothing and to give Doris her due she did keep the secret for a long time. Even when the incident was reported in the newspaper and she was tempted to say something she did not, and after three years she left her job in the workhouse and went to work at St Paul's school in Elswick which her children attended. She did not know that one of the teachers whom the children addressed as Mrs Reed was Cyril's daughter. If she had known she would have tried out her idea of getting money for keeping a family secret.

# Chapter 5

It was on one of the days when she was a little late in finishing her morning cleaning duties and was leaving as the children arrived at school that she could not help noticing a very pretty little girl with beautiful ash blonde, very curly, thick hair. She was chattering away and had a very expressive face, and you could not help noticing her big blue eyes. Those eyes and the ash blonde colour of her hair reminded Doris of that beautiful baby girl who had been left on the step of the workhouse a few years ago. She knew the foundling had been adopted and an idea formed in her mind. Could this attractive little girl possibly be the foundling baby. It could just be a coincidence, but she intended to find out. Her thoughts went into overdrive. What if she was the only one who knew the truth about the woman and the abandoned baby, and what if that baby was actually Cyril's baby? Did he even know about it? If he knew, why was Muriel on her own that morning? He would surely have been with her. There were questions to be asked and she wanted answers. If that baby was Cyril's baby, he had a right to know. She had to put her scheming into action.

Doris was a gossip as everybody knew and she was not popular as a result, but she envisaged being very popular if she had a big gossip story to tell. She might even be in the papers. It was obviously too late now to claim the reward that had been on offer for information at the time of the incident, but it would be enough reward to be the centre of attention when she told her story. She lost no time in confronting that little girl and calling her a workhouse baby. The little girl cried but nothing came of her attempts to hurt her and find out who she was and so she had to try again, adding very hurtful words like dirty and smelly. She even got her own children to help her to shout out the rude unkind words, which was a despicable thing to do. This time she had the satisfaction of making Annabel very upset indeed. Doris thought she might have gone too far. It actually occurred to her that if someone had done that to her children, she would have been very angry indeed, and taken the matter to the headteacher.

When Cyril saw how upset Annabel was for a second time coming out of school he was angry, and his instinct was to take her back into school and confront the headteacher, but he decided to tell Eleanor as he had done the last time. As a teacher at that school, she would know what to do. Eleanor listened carefully to what Cyril was saying to her and was very perturbed. This name calling was going on too long and she had to do something about it. When she went into school the day after Cyril had told her about Annabel and the bullies, because that is what they were, she was determined to get to the bottom of the problem. She asked the headteacher if she could gather the children in the school hall to talk to them, having first told her why she wanted to do that. She told the pupils about the name calling, describing it as a very unkind thing to do. She asked if anyone would own up to it although she was not expecting anyone to do so.

'If you cannot own up to it then you know it is very wrong,' Eleanor continued, 'and the headteacher and I are very disappointed with those people. Remember what the teachers are always telling you. Treat other children as you would like to be treated yourself. Now go back to your classrooms and if there is any more of this nonsense then there will be punishment and letters sent out to parents.'

Now Eleanor was more determined than ever to find out the person responsible for the name calling. It had to be an adult because children would not concern themselves with something like a workhouse. It was beyond their experience.

One evening she stayed behind after school to do some work and waited for the cleaning staff to arrive. There were four of them, one of whom seemed to have poor sight because she wore spectacles and screwed her eyes up in a most unattractive way when she was speaking or listening to someone else. Eleanor hovered around the cleaners on the pretext that she had to report that one of the classrooms would need cleaning thoroughly because someone had been very sick indeed. There was chickenpox in the school and cleanliness was of utmost importance to avoid more infections. The cleaner who wore spectacles and whom the others called Doris said she was used to cleaning up sick because she had once worked in the Workhouse and sickness was very common in there. The manager had a very high standard of cleanliness and inspected the workhouse every day. Unwittingly Doris had given the information Eleanor wanted. This was the woman who knew about workhouses. She now had to find out why this woman was picking on Annabel with her nasty taunts and so she kept on probing.

'Did you enjoy working at the workhouse, Doris? I would have thought it would be rather depressing.'

'It was at times,' Doris replied, 'but there were always new people arriving and leaving, which livened up the day. We had some real characters to deal with and some I did not like at all. They deserved their fate, but there were others who were genuine in their need, and you felt sorry for them. Workhouses are definitely not the best places in which to live.' She went on to say , that she had seen women sobbing uncontrollably as they desperately tried to do the hard tasks which they had been told to do to earn their keep and she had even seen men cry as they fretted about the position in which they had put their family. Worst of all though were the children who were separated from their parents and were desperately unhappy and neglected. 'It was very hard to be positive in a workhouse,' Doris said. 'Many of those who lived there were so poor that they were never allowed to leave. I thought myself to be quite tough but even I was disgusted and very upset at some of the things that happened in the workhouse and that is why I eventually had to leave my job there.

'There was one instance which surprised and shocked everyone.' Doris continued because she was enjoying telling the tale to an audience and being the centre of attention. 'One of the staff opened the front door one morning to find a tiny baby on the doorstep. It could only have been a few or even one day old, but it was well wrapped up in a beautiful hand knitted shawl and was very clean and obviously well fed. A baby so well cared for had never been left there before and never since I should think. The manager was sure someone would come back for the baby who had been found to be a girl, but no-one ever did. There was even a newspaper article asking for help and offering a reward if anyone could identify the baby, but no-one came forward and the baby was eventually put up for adoption. We were all sad about it really because that baby deserved her real mother. She was beautiful. I would have taken her home myself if that had been allowed and I have often wondered where she is now.'

'That is some story, Doris, if I may call you that,' Eleanor said with some concern. 'Did you ever make further inquiries about her whereabouts?'

'No,' Doris replied, 'though I was tempted sometimes.'

'Doris,' one of the other cleaners called Annie said. 'How long ago was that incident you are talking about, because I think you should leave well alone. It is really not your business.'

'I know,' Doris said, 'but I am still curious about it even though it was about eight years ago.'

'I agree with Annie, Doris,' Eleanor said. 'You do not need to concern yourself with that baby. She will undoubtedly be living happily with a new family now.'

The cleaners dispersed at that point to their various cleaning duties and Eleanor made her way home feeling very wretched. It was very bad news that someone else knew about the abandoned baby. Doris could be a threat to her family because she was well known for making trouble. Eleanor had to prevent Doris from talking about the incident, but she had no idea how she was going to do that.

A few days later a little girl in her class came to see her. She said that she was worrying about a little girl in another class because she had found her in the corner of the play yard 'crying her eyes out'. She thought the girl's name was Annabel.

Eleanor went to find Annabel who told her between her sobs that children were calling her names all the time now.

'Enough is enough,' Eleanor thought to herself. She would have to act now. She went to see Doris immediately after school and demanded to know why she was targeting Annabel with her cruel remarks about a workhouse.

'Why have you come to me?' Doris wanted to know.

'Because you are the person who worked in the Workhouse and our pupils have no experience of a workhouse and so would not use that word.'

Doris refused to admit that she was the source of the nasty name calling, but Eleanor gave her a warning that if there was any future occurrence of the name calling, she would be forced to take the matter further and it would not be pleasant. It could mean that she would lose her job and be asked to remove her children from the school.

Doris was frightened by Eleanor's words. She could not afford to lose her job and her husband would be very angry if she did. He would also be very angry if his children had to be taken out of the school because they were doing well there, and questions would be asked if they had to leave the school. Doris knew now that she had gone too far and very sensibly took Eleanor's advice and never incited any more name calling. She would have to think of another way to find out if that pretty little girl was the baby left on the workhouse step. Something was certainly not right but she would leave the matter alone for a while. Things settled down and for Annabel school was once again a happy place.

# Chapter 6

Eleanor was able to enjoy the last weeks of teaching there before she left to have her baby. The day she left she was overwhelmed with flowers and gifts from children, parents, friends and staff and she had to promise to take the baby into school to show everybody. Eleanor was a good teacher and very popular with the pupils. She would be greatly missed.

When she left school, she only had three weeks to wait until the birth of her baby. She was glad to have time to rest because she tired easily now that her pregnancy was so advanced, but nothing could prevent her and Tom getting more and more excited as they waited for their baby's birth. Five weeks later Eleanor went into labour and she gave birth to a beautiful baby girl. Tom and Eleanor were overjoyed and to them she was definitely the most perfect baby that had ever been born. When Tom wrapped his arms around Eleanor and their new baby daughter, he felt the proudest man on earth. His love for them both was overwhelming, and the love which Eleanor felt for her daughter, when she was put into her arms by the midwife in attendance, was for her the most precious moment of her life and she was sure she would remember it forever. It was almost as if she had been lifted to another sphere of life and she was being given a very precious gift, from which she never wanted to be parted. She wondered if that was what was meant by a spiritual experience! She felt a tremendous sense of protection for her baby and was looking forward to nurturing her and caring for her in the years to come. They were now a family of three and the future looked very good indeed. Eleanor had one regret and that was that her mother did not live to see her first grandchild. At the same time though, having given birth herself she wondered how her mother could possibly have abandoned her own child whom she had carried within her for nine months. She must have been in a highly emotional state and yet she had never mentioned that baby again. It was beyond belief.

The first weeks and months of being a mum were wonderful but very busy. There was more to bringing up a baby than Eleanor had realised. She seemed to be always washing delicate baby clothes, changing nappies, feeding the baby, shopping, making meals for herself and Tom, as well as all the other household chores and somehow the days flew past. Her favourite day was when, on fine days she met up with other young mums in Leazes Park, the first public park to be opened in Newcastle, and talked about babies and laughed at their own inadequacies or listened to one another's joys and fears of motherhood. Tom and she had decided to call their baby daughter Elizabeth Muriel and they watched her development with delight. Every night when Tom came in from school, he wanted to hear all about Eleanor's day with their baby. He was the best father Elizabeth could have. Every new movement or sound she made was noted and there was great excitement when instead of a 'windy' smile she started to really smile and take notice of what she saw around her. Being teachers, her development was of great interest to her parents, and she met every one of her 'milestones' with top marks as far as they were concerned. Grandfather Cyril was of course delighted with his first grandchild and was very touched that Eleanor had given her baby Muriel as her second name. Muriel would have loved that. Her four uncles made a great fuss of their new niece.

Only Benjamin, the youngest brother, was married. He had married Victoria in 1899, the year after Eleanor married Tom. Eleanor was especially pleased about the marriage because she was very close to Benjamin, having helped him with his lack of confidence and health problems when they were younger. She really liked Victoria and they had become good friends. Harry had a serious girlfriend as did Frank, but James said that he did not want to marry as he was totally committed to his work as a doctor and even said that he was planning to work abroad in another country eventually, to help people and children who were poor and sick with many ailments, which they could not understand or do anything about.

A frequent visitor to Tom and Eleanor's home was Annabel. She thought Elizabeth was the best baby in all the world and delighted in spending time with her. She talked to her, made funny faces, helped her to shake her rattles and play with her toys as she grew older. Babies always respond very well to other children and Elizabeth would gurgle and smile at Annabel all the time. It was a joy to see them together. Annabel was the first one to see Elizabeth trying to crawl and she ran straight into the kitchen where Eleanor was making tea to tell her about Elizabeth's latest achievement. She confided to Eleanor that she would love a sister or brother but meanwhile she was pretending that Elizabeth was her sister. Phillip, Ella and Annabel continued to be like family members of Cyril's family. They all had a wonderful celebration of Christmas at Cyril's house when Elizabeth was five months old. It was the first time they had had a baby in the house at Christmas and this made it special. It was good that their house at Summerhill was a large house because it was filled to capacity that Christmas with Cyril, the three older brothers and their girlfriends, Benjamin and Victoria, Phillip, Ella, Annabel and Tom's parents who greatly enjoyed spending time with their son and all Eleanor's family. They admitted to one another at times that when Tom first got to know Eleanor, they had had reservations about Eleanor (no woman was good enough for their son), but were very ashamed now to have had such thoughts because she was the very best wife their son could have had and was certainly a wonderful mother for their grandchild. Their son could not have married a lovelier girl than Eleanor and they were so appreciative of the warm welcome they always had from her family. That Christmas spent with their first grandchild and Eleanor's large family was magical for them. To see their son so happy was the best feeling in the world.

Tom had endless patience with his daughter and with Annabel who spent a lot of time in their house playing with Elizabeth. She was such a bright interesting happy little girl who was a joy to know. Tom was interested in music and one of the things he loved to hear was Annabel singing little songs to Elizabeth. She had a lovely singing voice and Elizabeth always responded with a delightful toothless grin and an appreciative gurgle, and even seemed to wave her arms about in time to the music. Eleanor and Tom both felt that Annabel's singing voice was a gift and that when she was older it could perhaps be trained. Eleanor did not enthuse about the singing voice too much because she knew that Annabel must have inherited it from her mother Muriel and that would be difficult to explain. Little seeds of doubt were beginning to take root in Cyril's mind. He was thinking workhouse, baby on step, ash blonde very curly hair, big blue eyes and beautiful singing voice. The doorstep baby would be Annabel's age now. Could there be a connection? Surely not and he dismissed the thought because that would mean that Annabel was his child, which could not possibly be true. There must be some other explanation but what it was he could never have imagined.

# Chapter 7

E leanor and Tom wanted Elizabeth christened at Easter 1901 when she would be eight months old. They had meant to have her christened much sooner, but they had been so busy with their new roles of being parents that time had passed by without them noticing it, until now. The nearest church to where they lived was St. Matthew's Church, just off the West Road, and Eleanor made arrangements with the vicar there for the christening to take place. He suggested that the christening could take place during one of the services and Tom and Eleanor agreed. This meant there would be extra people in attendance, as well as the family, but that was not a problem. Annabel in 1901 was almost 11 years old and was going to be one of the godparents. She looked very smart and pretty on the day. Frank and Harry and James were all going to be godparents also, as was Ella, Annabel's mother. Tom's parents, who were proud grandparents, were in the christening party and they were very surprised and dismayed by what happened next.

Unbeknown to Eleanor and her family, Doris the school cleaner was in the congregation that day with her three children and husband. The congregation were blissfully ignorant of what Doris was about to say.

As people turned in their seats to face the font for the baptism, a loud whisper was heard. It was Doris pointing a finger at Annabel and saying, 'Arthur, that is the little girl I was telling you about.'

'Telling me what,' Arthur said for all to hear.

'You remember, the Workhouse Baby.'

The voice could be clearly heard because Arthur was more than a little deaf and Doris had to speak quite loudly in order to make him hear. Eleanor's cheeks coloured bright red. She was mortified and worse was to come when the vicar announced that the name of the baby was Elizabeth Muriel.

Doris could be heard again saying, 'There you are, Arthur, I knew I was right. Muriel was the name of the woman I saw leaving her baby on the workhouse step.'

There was a loud gasp from the congregation.

The vicar tried desperately to bring order when everyone started talking and voices rose higher and higher. In the end he found it necessary to ask members of the congregation to leave and the christening continued without them., Cyril, Tom, Eleanor, James, Frank, Harry and Kate, Benjamin and Victoria who was heavily pregnant with her first baby. Phillip Ella, Annabel and Tom's parents stood in shock and bewilderment and Annabel began to cry uncontrollably.

'It is happening again,' she sobbed, 'and I still do not know what workhouse means. That lady who shouted out in church works at our school but why does she keep on calling me a workhouse baby?'

Eleanor was shaking as she said, 'We are going to find out what she means, Annabel, but just for now stop crying and we will all go home for a special lunch. You can play with the baby while I am laying the table and putting final touches to the lunch. You always enjoy playing with Elizabeth.'

It was a very subdued group of people who returned home that day. It had been going to be a happy family celebration, but it had been a very uncomfortable occasion and explanations would have to be given.

Cyril was very concerned. There must be a reason for that woman's unkind and ridiculous words. He would have to find out because she seemed to be attacking his family. He spoke first to Eleanor and asked if she knew any reason why Annabel was being connected with the workhouse.

'No, Father,' she said with gritted teeth, 'but I intend to find out.'

Phillip and Ella were very upset after the christening, as were Tom's parents. It was a very bizarre situation. Why had that woman accused Annabel of being a workhouse baby? It was ridiculous and they would have to go and see the Headteacher. Eleanor of course was horrified. She had protected her family from knowing the truth for 11 years and she wanted it to stay that way. Too many people would have their lives turned upside down if the truth came out. Her father was already suspicious and now Ella and Phillip had questions they wanted to ask, and as for Tom's parents she did not dare ask how they felt. They worshipped regularly at St. Mary's Cathedral ever since Tom and Eleanor had taken them there in the early days of their friendship. They had found the people very welcoming and loved worshipping God in such a beautiful church.

Two weeks after the christening Eleanor wheeled Elizabeth's pram purposefully into the school. She had promised to take the baby into school sometime but today that was not her only purpose. She was going to sort out the matter with Doris and this time she was determined to succeed. She had a lovely afternoon. Everyone admired Elizabeth and the children made a great fuss of her much to the baby's delight. She was sitting up now of course and becoming more and more aware of the world around her and was very responsive to the children talking and smiling at her. She loved the attention. When Annabel appeared, she beamed and laughed, and one of the children asked if she was Annabel's sister to which Annabel replied, 'I really wish she was. I would love a brother or sister.' Ella and Phillip would have loved to have a child of their own but sadly they could not, and they did not want to adopt another child. They adored Annabel and had never felt the need for a second adopted child.

At the end of the afternoon Eleanor waited for Doris to arrive at the school for her cleaning duties. When she saw Doris, the latter had the grace to look discomfited. She had not known that Eleanor, or Mrs Reed as she was called in school, was in any way related to Cyril and Muriel or she would have been much more careful in what she had said at the christening.

Eleanor wanted to be angry with Doris, but she knew from experience that angry words just made a situation worse. She could not cope with confrontations and so she said politely, 'Doris, please can you tell me why you persist in making Annabel Gibson so miserable at school with your name calling? I must know. You disrupted the christening of my baby and completely spoiled what should have been a very happy occasion.'

Doris did not know what to say, but eventually she apologised for her behaviour at the christening and then went on to say, 'Mrs Reed, I knew Cyril, your father, and Muriel, your mother, from my younger days and I am sure it was she whom I saw leaving a baby on the Workhouse front step. That little girl in the school called Annabel is the age that that baby would be today, and she has the same blonde, thick curly hair as your mother Muriel. When I heard in church that the baby had Muriel as her second name, I was sure I was right. Tell me, am I right in thinking you know about the workhouse and the abandoned baby?'

Eleanor really had to think now about her answer. She could not own up to knowing about the abandoned baby. It would have many repercussions if she did. On the other hand, she did not want to lie.

It was becoming increasingly obvious that her mother had been seen that fateful morning by someone other than herself and it was a grim realisation. Doris could make a lot of trouble if people believed what she was saying but she had to answer Muriel's question.

'Doris, I am not related to Annabel. She is the daughter of two very good friends of ours and I know nothing about a workhouse, but you are right in that my mother was called Muriel. It was very unfortunate that she died just after my wedding in 1898 and I had to come home early from my honeymoon. I wonder why you are so interested in Muriel, my mother. You obviously, from what you say, knew my father but you did not know my mother very well. I think you are muddling her up with someone else, because I just know my mother would never have abandoned her baby. I am one of five siblings and my mother loved us all very dearly. I am really upset that you are spreading gossip about her. It is very unkind.'

'I understand what you are saying, Mrs Reed, but I am very sure that it was Muriel I saw leaving a baby on the workhouse step.'

'Think carefully, Doris. You said it was very early in the morning, when it can be just half light. I notice that you wear spectacles, with thick lenses which could mean that your vision is not clear, especially from a distance and you could have been mistaken about the person you saw. There is no way you could prove that it was my mother because as I have already told you she died several years ago.'

Doris was now wavering and having doubts about her story and whether she should have said anything at all about a workhouse baby. 'I am so sorry, Mrs Reed, that I have upset you. You are right about my eyesight. I do not always see very well in the morning. I have to rub my eyes every morning because they are blurry. I promise not to bring this matter up again and I promise not to upset that lovely little girl anymore.'

'Thank you for that, Doris. Annabel may be adopted but she could not be more loved than if our friends were the birth parents. She does not deserve to be made unhappy by you, and so this matter is closed, and if I hear any more about it, I will take the matter further. The police have a dim view of people who harass others, so be warned.'

Doris wanted to say one more thing to Eleanor. She could not resist it.

'Please would you tell your father, Mrs Reed, that Doris thinks he is a very handsome man. In fact, he is even better looking now than when he was a young man.' That will give him something to think about, Doris thought.

# Chapter 8

Doris was pleased with herself. She was now absolutely sure that it was Muriel and Cyril's baby who had been abandoned, despite what Eleanor had said and it was Muriel the baby's mother who had abandoned her. It was scandalous and she was not going to forget it ever. It was obvious too that Cyril knew nothing about it. One way or another she was going to make sure that he got to know. In her mind he deserved to be upset and miserable for not taking notice of her when they worked at the factory and ignoring her when she moved to Sandhill. He was bound to have remembered her from their school days. She felt rejected and that was not a nice feeling.

Eleanor's talk with Doris did not convince her that that was the end of the matter. She had a feeling that Doris would make it her business to find out more about Muriel and the baby her father knew nothing about.

Eleanor wondered what her father thought about it all and the next time she saw him she was not too surprised when he asked her why the woman in church that day of the christening, had said what she did.

'Do not worry about it, Father. She is just one of those people who likes trouble and, unfortunately, for some reason she has targeted Annabel. The workhouse is where she worked before her marriage, and I think what she saw there has confused her thought processes. She has promised me that her bad behaviour will stop from now on. By the way, she knew your name, and what's more she said I had to tell you that you are still a very handsome man.'

'I can assure you I have no idea who she is, Eleanor, and I do not want to know her after making all that trouble for Annabel,' was Cyril's reply.

Ironically Cyril loved Annabel as if she were his own! He enjoyed having children around him and loved the company of Annabel and Elizabeth. He was further delighted when Jack his grandson was born in 1902. Elizabeth was then two and a half years old and getting into all sorts of mischief. She was great fun and such a chatterbox. Her best friend was Annabel who loved playing games with her. Their favourite game was hide and seek. Annabel always found some great places to hide, and Elizabeth squealed with delight when she discovered her hiding place. They were happy times, which would always be remembered.

Annabel was going to secondary school soon and seemed to be growing up too quickly. She still enjoyed playing with Elizabeth and she still loved dolls and had lots of them. She and Elizabeth loved putting their dolls in and out of their prams and taking them for walks. Elizabeth's other gran, Tom's mother, had knitted some lovely clothes for the dollies Their dolls' prams were not 'posh' because toys were not readily available at the beginning of the 20th century. Cyril had a friend who was a joiner and loved working with wood and he asked his friend if there was any possibility of him being able to make two dolls' prams. Cyril was not at all sure if it was possible to make prams out of wood, but his friend was happy to try and a few weeks later Annabel and Elizabeth each had a little wooden pram in which to put their dolls. They played 'Mothers and Dolls and Prams' for hours and spent a lot of time dressing and undressing their dolls. When Eleanor took Jack out in his pram, Annabel and Elizabeth went with her pushing their 'babies' in their prams, although it seemed to take much longer to get anywhere. If they went to Leazes Park, it was only a short walk, and the girls enjoyed throwing their balls around or to each other. Jack used to watch them from his pram and chuckle and wave his arms around. No doubt when he was older, he would love kicking a ball in the park. The summer of 1902 passed very happily, and Doris and her taunts were forgotten. Surely the past could not hurt them now.

Annabel started her new school in September 1902. She was 11 now and her parents had decided to send her to Dame Allan's school on the recommendation of Eleanor who had been educated there, as had her brothers. St Paul's school had given a very good account of Annabel when she left there and said they would be very sorry to lose her because it was obvious that she loved learning and was very hard working. At her new school Annabel particularly enjoyed music lessons and her music teacher thought her beautiful singing voice was a definite gift and told her parents that with their permission she would like to find someone who would train Annabel's voice. Phillip and Ella told the teacher that they would like her to go ahead with that because they too appreciated the quality of her voice and had always thought that it should be trained This was arranged by the music teacher when Annabel was 13 and she absolutely loved her singing lessons. She was settling in very well at her new school and over the next few months Annabel flourished into a solo singer who was much sought after for concerts and musical performances. She had no fear in front of an audience and absolutely loved being a performer. How Cyril wished Muriel could have lived to hear this little girl singing and entertaining with her beautiful voice. He remembered Muriel telling him that when she was a little girl she used to sing for her mother's friends when they came to her house and Muriel was very proud of one of the comments made by one of those friends. She had said to Muriel, 'You sing like an angel.'

# Chapter 9

Cyril missed meeting Annabel out of St Paul's school, but he was pleased that she was growing up to be a confident, independent young lady and certainly a very pretty one. He could see how much she was enjoying her new school and how hard she was working. Her parents had shown by example the rewards of working hard and Annabel wanted to attain a high standard in her schoolwork so that she could get a good job when she was older. Phillip and Ella were so proud of her as of course were Cyril, Eleanor and Tom. All her unhappiness at St Paul's school was safely in the past. Eleanor hoped her family would not come into contact with Doris again, but unfortunately that was not to be.

Cyril still went out for his afternoon walk even though there was no-one to collect from school. It would not be long before Elizabeth started school and he would be needed again, but he liked walking and almost every time took the same route, which was up the West Road as far as the Workhouse and then down one of the many side streets back to Summerhill. Every time he passed the workhouse, he thought of the taunts Annabel had endured. He still had the feeling that there was something he did not know and which he was not being told. Eleanor had assured him that all was well, but it still niggled at the back of his mind.

One day he was taking his normal route back to Summerhill down a side street when a woman shouted out at him from her garden.

'It is you, Cyril, I am sure. Do you remember me?'

Cyril saw to his horror that it was that dreadful woman from the school who had made a fuss at the christening. He still had not forgiven that.

'Yes, I am called Cyril, but no, I do not know who you are,' Cyril replied.

'I know you, Cyril. You and I went to the same school in Byker, and then when we left, we both worked at the same factory in the Ouseburn Valley. You must remember the Maling Potteries in the Ouseburn Valley in Byker, where we worked in our teens. I used to think you were so good looking in those days and I must say that you have kept your looks. You are a handsome man even now, and in those days, I don't mind telling you that I had a crush on you,' Doris said cheekily.

Cyril could not help smiling. He liked compliments even from this rather coarse woman. He did, however, have some questions for her and said, 'You are the lady who shouted out at my grandaughter's christening, aren't you?'

'Yes, I am, and I am very sorry about that. I realise that I was very rude,' Doris replied.

'Apology accepted,' Cyril said, 'but tell me one thing. Why did the name Muriel bother you, Doris? Did you know my wife?'

'Why don't you come in for a cup of tea and I will tell you,' Doris replied.

Cyril was hesitant but decided to accept her invitation. He was curious about her reasons for saying what she did. Doris reminded him again that they had worked in the same pottery in the Ouseburn Valley at Byker when they left school. It was the Maling Pottery and was considered to be the best pottery of all those who had premises in the Ouseburn Valley. The conversation flowed as they reminisced about Byker and the school they had attended there and their workdays in the Maling factory. Doris told him how much she had enjoyed working in that pottery.

Doris loved to talk and was very happy filling in the details of the time they worked together at Maling's Pottery where she first met him.

'I have heard that exciting things are happening now at the Maling Pottery. When you and I worked there we made mainly domestic ware and things which were of use for local working people, such as large jars to contain jam and marmalade. Robert Maling was the owner then and he was not creative but a good businessman. Do you remember him, Cyril? He was a kind boss but his son Christopher Robert Maling took over from him in the 1850s and he was ambitious. He took the firm to a whole new level. He devised a way to make pottery containers by machine which was a lot quicker than by hand and of course that speeded up the production process and soon orders were flooding in from manufacturers of goods such as marmalade, meat and fish pastes, ointments and printing inks, all of which needed the suitable containers that Maling Potteries could provide. My mother bought some marmalade in a Keilder's jar made by Maling. You can still buy those Keilder jars, Cyril. They are considered to be the best.

'Even better though is that in the 1890s I heard that Maling's employed their first designer and imported porcelain from other potteries which they decorated and sold under their name. After that it was not long before the quality of the Maling pottery was so good that it was being sold in big stores like Harrods in London. Maling Pottery could fetch a good price and was valuable.'

Eventually, although Doris and Cyril could not know it then, competition from more modern and streamlined potteries resulted in Maling's Pottery closing in 1963. In two centuries, it had produced over 16,500 patterns and items which ranged from simple kitchen wares such as pudding basins to highly gilded lustred and enamel ware.

'You and I, Cyril played a part in Maling's success by working for them, and we should be proud of that. Those were good days, Cyril, when we were young and carefree, but I have talked long enough. Tell me more about your family, but just one more thing. You might have wondered why I live in the West End of Newcastle now. My father got a new job in Lord Armstrong's shipyard at Elswick, and we moved to the Sandhill area. It was pure chance that I saw you with a young lady whom I later found out was your wife. Someone told me that she was called Muriel and that answers your question, Cyril. Now, Cyril, it is your turn to tell me a little about yourself. One thing I know about you is that you are a very good listener. I am quite breathless after my long account of myself and believe it or not there is quite a lot more to be told.'

Cyril of course enjoyed nothing better than talking about his family. He was really enjoying this time spent with Doris. She was very friendly and easy to talk to, and he felt very relaxed. He told her all about his four sons and his only daughter Eleanor, whom she now knew was a teacher at the school where she was working as a cleaner. He told her all about Eleanor's wedding and the lovely day they all had and the happiness he and Muriel felt that she was marrying such a nice young man who loved her very much indeed.

Cyril then had to tell her the dreadful event that followed when Muriel died very unexpectedly the next day. His eyes filled with tears and Doris rested her hand on his arm in support. She felt very sorry, but it was clear that he knew nothing about Muriel leaving a baby on the workhouse step. Why was that she asked herself? There was definitely a mystery there and she would have to find out what it was, but it was proving difficult to do that.

Meanwhile Cyril was asking her about her family. He had seen her at the christening with her husband and three children. She told him that her husband was only at the christening so that her neighbours would think they were still married but they were actually in the middle of divorce proceedings and her husband did not live with her. She was finding it very difficult to make ends meet and the children were getting more and more difficult to control. Their father took no interest in them and contributed less and less to their upkeep. They seemed to be forever asking for money and were very rude to her when she could not give it to them. She could not wait until they were old enough to leave school and get paid work so that they could contribute to the family income. Now it was Cyril's turn to lay a hand on her arm to show his support.

# Chapter 10

Cyril had enjoyed his afternoon with Doris so that when Doris asked him to call the next week while on his daily walk he was pleased to do so and soon it became a weekly date to which he looked forward. Doris had turned out to be a good friend and he enjoyed her company very much. He could not believe he had ever felt some hatred of her. She had apologised for her rudeness at the christening and that was good enough for him. She was such a good listener and seemed genuinely interested in his family. Cyril never doubted that she was sincere in her interest, but of course there was a reason for it.

Doris was aware that Cyril was a successful businessman. She had been making enquiries after the christening episode and she had found out that he lived in Summerhill in one of the bigger houses there, which only the wealthy could afford. In her deliberations on the subject, she imagined herself the mistress of a house in Summerhill and the envy of her neighbours in Elswick. She knew from Cyril that his family all had good jobs and they would be a good influence on her children who were causing quite a lot of trouble the older they grew. Her oldest son at secondary school had narrowly missed going to prison for one of his misdemeanours. Her daughter, now a teenager, was out with her boyfriend every night and the youngest son had been reported to the police for his bad behaviour and bad language. He was in the top class at St Paul's school and already had a very bad reputation. All this was made worse by the fact that she was getting into debt. It was all getting too much for her and she needed someone in her life who could give her money and who could help her to control her children. Cyril would be her ideal man.

As the weeks went by Doris tried every way she could, to beguile Cyril. She flattered him all the time and said how marvellous it was that his family had done so well which must be down to the way they were brought up. She said how fortunate Muriel had been to have such a good husband as himself and she told him what a wonderful cook she was and how she could provide good nutritious meals for any amount of people. As the weeks went by Doris began to realise that Cyril was completely unimpressed by her or her fine words. It was obvious that Cyril was perfectly content with his life as it was, and he was certainly not looking for a companion, and least of all for a wife. As far as he was concerned, no-one could compare to Muriel. It had never occurred to him for one moment that Doris was interested in a relationship with him. He would never marry again. He did, however, recognise Doris's kindness to him, and he appreciated her hospitality. Indeed, he praised her for those attributes, and was rewarded with a dazzling smile from her thickly coated red lips. It was a pity about the gaps in her front teeth because otherwise she could have been quite pretty.

It took some time, but Doris did finally realise that all her efforts to ensnare Cyril were to no avail and she became increasingly angry about it. Blackmail was now out of the question. She could see that he would not accept that, and she could find herself in big trouble, but in her twisted way she wanted to punish this man for being so loyal to a woman like Muriel who gave away his child. She could not imagine herself doing such a wicked thing, though she had to admit that she had said and done things that were wrong. Cyril had a right to know what Muriel had done, because at the moment he was oblivious of the truth. She had actually seen Muriel leaving her baby at the workhouse. The big question was why Cyril did not know anything about it. If she could convince him that Muriel had abandoned his baby, there could be a chance that he would turn to her for comfort, and they might even have a future together. Little by little she began planting seeds of doubt in Cyril's mind.

'How many children did you say you had, Cyril?' Doris asked him one afternoon.

'I think I have already told you,' he replied, 'Muriel and I had five children, four sons and one daughter. You must remember me saying how thrilled we were when our fifth child was a daughter.'

'You only have one daughter, did you say. Are you sure about that? I wonder what you would have thought about a second daughter?' Doris dared to say.

'It would have been a surprise but a very nice one, I have to say,' Cyril said, wondering why Doris was questioning him in this way.

Doris continued, 'If I had been Muriel, I would have liked to try for another daughter.'

'No, Doris. We felt our family was complete when Eleanor was born, and we never considered having any more babies. Five children were quite enough and my goodness I am so proud of them. They have all grown up to be admirable young people.'

Doris felt a sharp stab of jealousy. It was alright for people with money. She had had to work for every bit of money she had, and she had been stupid enough to marry a lazy, workshy man who could never have given her the money she craved. She was well rid of him and was looking for a man of wealth to raise her status and help her to live her dream of being a rich woman. Cyril would have been her ideal man. She continued her attack.

'I wonder what you would have said, Cyril, if Muriel told you she was pregnant again and you had had another daughter.'

Cyril was now becoming irritated with this conversation. Where was it leading, he wondered?

'Doris, why don't we talk about something else before I leave. I might not see you next week because apparently my daughter has something planned for me. I will be back as soon as I can, but I really must go because Eleanor has invited me for tea to discuss something, and I do not want to be late.'

Cyril left her house rather hurriedly. Doris sensed that Cyril was displeased. She had certainly made him feel uncomfortable and she was glad. She really was not attracted to him physically at all. It was all a big pretence. She was only interested in him financially. There clearly was no romance on his part and she realised there never would be. It made her angry somehow that he was rejecting her when he had been very glad of her listening ear. She could tell that he was now tiring of her company, and she may not get the chance to talk to him again. The only thing she could do now was spread rumours about Muriel and hurt him that way. He would regret one day that he had ever met her and that would be his punishment.

# Chapter 11

Cyril had a lot to think about as he walked home that
evening and he could not help feeling uneasy. Why
had Doris brought up the subject of babies? He had that
feeling again that there was something he was not being told.
Doris had seemed determined to ask him those questions,
but why? Perhaps it was a good thing that his daughter had
something she wanted him to do because the truth was that
he had sensed a change in Doris's manner towards him
that afternoon. She was even a little hostile in her attitude
towards him and he had already made up his mind not to
visit her again. In any case he could spend more time with
Elizabeth and Jack. It would be helping Eleanor if he took
the children for walks or even did her shopping. He was
very glad that he had a good relationship with his daughter
Eleanor, and again he could not help thinking how much
Muriel would have enjoyed her grandchildren. It was nearly
five years since Muriel had died and he still missed her very

much. It was rather uncanny how much alike Annabel and Muriel were. They both had ash blonde hair and big blue eyes, and according to Eleanor, Annabel had a lovely singing voice too. Muriel had also had a beautiful singing voice.

Cyril knew it could only be coincidence but nevertheless he looked upon Annabel as an adopted granddaughter and she always called him Grandpa Cyril. Elizabeth, his other granddaughter, also had a lovely singing voice which she must have inherited from Muriel. Annabel and Elizabeth loved singing together especially when Grandpa Cyril asked them. Their favourite song was 'Jesus loves me this I know'. They had learnt it at Sunday School which they attended every Sunday at St. John's Church at the bottom of the West Road where it met with Grainger Street. Eleanor took them there every Sunday and they always looked forward to it and enjoyed it very much.

A man called Robert Raikes who was born in 1736 founded the Sunday School Movement and it became so strong that it pre-dated state schooling, which came later near the end of the 19th century. Robert Raikes was supported by clergyman who had realised that to have school on a Sunday was the best way to educate children. The reason for this was that on the other days of the week, children in the 18th and 19th centuries were expected to work, in order to earn money to give to their parents. Attendance on weekdays at the limited number of schools which were set up in the 19th century was therefore very erratic and meant that some children were never taught how to read or write. That is why Robert Raikes founded the Sunday School movement and attendance at these schools was very good. The Sunday schools were held in churches where clergymen who were considered learned men, could help with the education of these children. Clergyman were much more aware of the educational needs of children and gave importance to learning in the 19th century in a way that the general public did not. They were a great support to the Sunday Schools. The four key churches in Newcastle were the first to set up Sunday Schools in their churches, namely St. John's, at the bottom of the West Road; St Andrew's at Gallowgate, believed to be the oldest church in Newcastle; All Saints beside the Old River Tyne Bridge, the present day bridge not being built until 1928; and St Nicholas's beside the old Keep and Gatehouse. This church was made a Cathedral in 1882, the same year that Newcastle became a Diocese for the Church of England. Newcastle also changed status from a town to a city when St Nicholas's church became a cathedral..

It was good for children's education that things changed as the 19th century advanced and towards the end of the century education was taken very seriously, culminating in two Education Acts, one in 1870 and the other in 1880, making attendance at school compulsory. Many more schools were built and staffed by educated adults. Training colleges for teachers were being set up and education was considered very important. It was certainly much more organised by the turn of the century.

Annabel and Elizabeth loved singing the hymns and songs at Sunday School and because Grandpa Cyril spent most of Sunday at Elizabeth's house, he was there when they returned from Sunday School and always asked them to sing any of the new hymns or songs which they had learnt.

Their favourite hymn was 'All things bright and beautiful' and it quickly became a favourite of Grandpa Cyril. They were delighted when he got to know the words enough to join in with them. One of the teachers had told everybody that a lady called Cecil Frances Humphreys Alexander had written it sometime between 1818 and 1895 and it was set to a tune called 'Royal Oak'. She had been inspired to write the words by a verse in the first chapter of the Bible, describing the Creation of the World. 'And God saw everything he had made and behold it was very good.' (Genesis Chapter 1, verse 31.) One day Grandpa Cyril had got out his Bible and showed Annabel and Elizabeth where those words were written. It was a very big Bible and so heavy that neither of them could hold it. Grandpa told them that it was a Family Bible which was very old. The edges of the pages were gilt trimmed, and Grandpa told them that it had been used and read by many people who belonged to Grandpa and Grandma's family. It had lots of names written in the front and one day when Elizabeth could write her name really well, she could put her name in it. Annabel, of course, could write her name well now in her 'joined up' writing and she wanted to put her name in the Bible immediately, and although Grandpa tried to explain that only his family could put their name in it, he allowed her to write her name.

'Grandpa, you have always said I am like family to you so there is nothing wrong with me signing my name,' Annabel said.

Cyril did not yet know, of course, that Annabel was family She was perfectly entitled as it happened to put her name in the Bible and was doing just the right thing. After the signing of their names, Annabel and Elizabeth sang their favourite hymn again and their voices blended so perfectly to create a wonderful sound in perfect pitch, that tears began to run down Cyril's cheeks. He thought of Muriel and how proud she would have been that her granddaughter had inherited her own beautiful singing voice. When they sang for Eleanor she thought how proud her mother would have been of her granddaughter and her daughter. Cyril commented on more than one occasion that it was uncanny how many of Muriel's characteristics the two girls shared but never for a moment did he think they could be related in some way.

# Chapter 12

It had not gone unnoticed that Cyril was enjoying his afternoon walks and indeed Tom commented to Eleanor that her father seemed to have a spring in his step these days, so Eleanor followed this up by saying to Cyril:

'Father, you seem to be enjoying your daily afternoon walk because it is taking longer and longer. I think you are much happier these days.'

She and Tom were both glad about this because it had taken him a long time to get over Muriel's death. Eleanor might not have been quite so happy had she known whom Cyril was visiting on his walks. He had not told her about his visits to Doris's home, although he did say that he had met Doris a few times while out walking.

'Father, do be careful what you say to Doris because you know what a gossip she is. I do not like the idea of her gossiping about our family.' Eleanor was afraid that Doris would bring up the subject of the workhouse again and that could lead to trouble, especially if she talked about the time when she worked at the workhouse. Cyril could not understand why Eleanor was so concerned about gossip concerning their family. They were all respectable and had nothing to hide, as far as he knew, though he still sometimes had the feeling that there was something he was not being told.

He put all these thoughts aside as he approached Eleanor's house, on the day she had asked him to tea. It was a joy going there and as usual Elizabeth came running to meet him so that he could catch her and swing her up in the air and round and round. Today little Jack was sitting in his pram, but it would not be long before he too was running up for a swing. He smiled at his grandpa and gurgled a welcome. He really was a pleasant baby, and it was a joy to see how happy and secure both his grandchildren were. It was what all children deserved and somehow that image of an abandoned baby on the doorstep of a workhouse just would not go away.

Eleanor had some very happy news for Cyril. He was a grandfather for the third time. His son Benjamin and his wife Victoria had become proud parents of a beautiful baby son. They had called the baby Edward after the present King of England, Edward the 7th. Cyril was overjoyed for them. Benjamin had once been so shy and lacking in confidence and at one time was adamant that he would not get married, but he had grown into a confident, talented artist who would make a lovely father, and his son would hopefully inherit some of his father's artistic gifts. Cyril remembered how much he and Muriel had worried about Benjamin when he was young. His health gave cause for concern and he was not so academic as his three brothers and sister, but he had artistic talent which had developed over the years into professional success. Remarkably, his health had recovered to the extent that he was able to live a full active life enhanced of course by his choice of partner. Benjamin and Victoria had married in 1899, the year after Eleanor and Tom had married and they had lived with Cyril in his large Summerhill house for some time after their marriage, but after several months they had decided to move to the Lake District. The move was prompted because of their mutual interest in art. They were always looking for inspiration for their art and craft work and decided that living in the country would provide greater inspiration. Benjamin had always done a lot of reading when he was young. At the time it was a form of escapism for him because when he was engrossed in a book, he could forget his problems and worries. He was oblivious of the world around him when he was reading. The countryside would provide him with perfect surroundings for reading and would surely help to nurture his ambition to one day be a writer himself.

He and Victoria had bought a modest cottage near the picturesque Lakeland town of Keswick and had settled down to enjoy country life. Initially Victoria was going to find a job while Benjamin was going to paint and try to build up a business for their paintings and crafts, but this had not proved to be a viable way of life and they had both got jobs in the Pencil Mill Factory, which at the beginning of the 20th century was quickly becoming a great tourist attraction in Keswick and certainly a main source of employment. The Derwent Pencil Company produced pencils of a very high standard and became known nationally for the excellence of their products. Benjamin and Victoria liked the history of these pencils. It was all to do with Graphite deposits which were discovered around Keswick in the 16th Century and pencils were made at first in cottages until 1832 when the first pencil factory in the United Kingdom was opened in Keswick. Benjamin and Victoria made good use of the pencils with their artwork and of course they continued painting whenever they could, because painting was a way of life for them and very precious. There was so much to inspire them in their beautiful surroundings, and they enjoyed walking on the fells and following the abundance of woodland paths and trails which surrounded their home. Walking beside Lake Derwentwater was their favourite walk and one day they actually walked right round the lake. It took up most of the day when they did that because the scenery was so beautiful that they frequently stopped to admire it, and this slowed their pace considerably. They knew beyond doubt that they had made the right decision to move to this beautiful part of the world. They would have liked to climb at least one of the mountains, but although Benjamin's health was much better, he would not risk serious climbing. He would leave the mountains for their visitors to enjoy.

Benjamin had already begun to do some writing and had even begun to write poetry. He was very interested in learning more about the Lakeland Poets, all of whom drew inspiration from the beautiful mountains and landscapes of the Lake District. Poetry interested him because it was a good way to express emotions and feelings. The Lake Poets, as they were first called, were a group of English Poets who all lived in the Lake District in England in the first half of the

19th century. Among them were Samuel Taylor Coleridge, Robert Southey, Thomas De Quincy, Mary and Charles Lamb, Dorothy Wordsworth and her brother William, who is the most well-known. Benjamin found great pleasure in reading the poems of William Wordsworth. Victoria shared her husband's interest in the Lakeland Poets, and they were hoping to find out more about them when they were settled into their new home in the Lake District. They could also visit places where the poets had lived surrounded by the beauty of nature. Benjamin was so inspired by Wordsworth's poem about daffodils that he painted a picture of the 'host of daffodils' and it was so excellent that Victoria asked several people to their house to see it. This led to people asking Benjamin to paint a similar picture for them, and they were prepared to pay for it, which naturally was great news for the couple and their family income. Victoria was extremely proud of her husband.

William Wordsworth had written the Daffodil Poem after a walk in the countryside near Grasmere where he had lived with his sister Dorothy for nine years. On this particular walk with Dorothy, they had come across a field or 'host' of golden daffodils and their unique beauty had given him the inspiration to write the now very well-known and well-loved poem. The words of the first verse were etched on Benjamin's heart.

*"I wandered lonely as a cloud,*
*That floats on high o'er vales and hills.*
*When all at once I saw a crowd*
*A host of Golden Daffodils*

*Beside the lake, beneath the trees*
*Fluttering and dancing in the breeze."*

Benjamin and Victoria were united in finding out more about Wordsworth and he and Victoria visited 'Dove Cottage' in Grasmere, where William and his sister Dorothy had lived from 1799 to 1808 and they also went to Cockermouth where Wordsworth was born in 1770. It was not too far away from Grasmere on the outskirts of the Lake District. Ben admired William Wordsworth, not only for his poetry but the sentiment behind his work. Wordsworth felt it was his vocation to write poetry and he took it very seriously. He had said that he wanted to write poetry that would make the world a better place. It was those words which impressed Benjamin and which he chose to remember when he was writing his own poetry.

# Chapter 13

Ben's brothers Frank and Harry were frequent visitors to their brother's home, loving as they did to be out of doors. They thoroughly enjoyed walking on the fells and over time graduated to climbing the alluring mountains. Their enthusiasm for climbing increased over the months and they made good use of the books which were available then, giving advice about mountain climbing They began their climbing exploits on the fells in the area surrounding Keswick and Lake Bassenthwaite, namely Blencathra, Latrigg, Skiddaw, Causey Pike, Grisedale, Catbells, Walla Crag, and Castle Crag, none of which were high enough to require specified equipment or expert mountain knowledge. They did, however, get more adventurous and ventured further up into the Borrowdale Valley to Seathwaite from where they could climb Scafell Pike, the highest mountain in England. The climb was not an easy one. Great Gable was another challenge and for this they had to go to Wasdale in the western part of the Lake District. It was a much more remote area, but Great Gable lived up to its name for them, even though it was a difficult climb, and they certainly felt Great when they reached its summit. Sometime in the future they wanted to climb Helvellyn and tackle 'Striding Edge' which was part of the climb to its summit. It was a dangerous climb, but they enjoyed a challenge and James had said he would like to join them for that particular climb.

Ben and Victoria always welcomed the brothers warmly and greatly enjoyed their visits. Victoria was especially pleased when Harry began bringing his girlfriend Kate to Keswick because she was good female company, and they could enjoy easier walking routes together. Victoria secretly hoped that Harry and Kate would get engaged. She would love Kate for a sister-in-law. She and Kate became firm friends and later when Victoria became pregnant, she was especially glad to have some female company in whom she could confide and talk about, not only the joys but also the fears and anxieties which accompany pregnancy. Births in Victorian times were shrouded in anxiety which carried on into the early part of the 20th century and that is why Victoria could not help being anxious, but she need not have worried because all went according to plan and she was safely delivered of a beautiful son.

James, the oldest brother, was so busy with his work as a doctor that he could not spend as much time with Benjamin and Victoria as he would have liked. He enjoyed being out of doors just as much as his younger brothers and he would have liked to join them more than his work allowed. It was going to be difficult arranging a time when all the brothers were free together, in order to climb Helvellyn. James worked so hard at the hospital and did not get too much leave. He worked in the Newcastle Hospital when it was situated at Forth Banks, the area near the Central Station. It had been founded in 1751. When James went to work there in 1897, he knew that a decision had been made to build a new hospital for Newcastle to replace the old one at Forth Banks. The new hospital was to commemorate the year of Queen Victoria's Diamond Jubilee. £300,000 was raised to build this hospital and the corporation and Freemen of Newcastle provided 10 acres of land on the Castle Leazes Moor, which was a section of the Town Moor, a vast area of green land on the outskirts of Newcastle.

James, along with many citizens of Newcastle, was very excited when building commenced in 1900. It took six years to build and it was opened on the 11th of July in 1906 by King Edward VIIth. It was called the Royal Victoria Infirmary, but sadly Queen Victoria did not live to see the finished building and perhaps even open it, because she died in 1901. There is a special memorial to her just outside the main hospital entrance in the form of a white marble statue on top of a white pedestal. It is of Queen Victoria, in her younger days, dressed in her robes with an orb, sceptre and crown. James had the honour of working at the R.V.I. as it became known, for the rest of his life. He saw it grow and develop into a major, prestigious hospital of our country. He was proud to be part of a hospital which cared for the people of Newcastle and continued to grow, adapt and keep up to date with continuous advances in medical practice and technologies. He could not have known then that this hospital, the Royal

Victoria Infirmary, would grow to be internationally famous for its pioneering work in almost all forms of medicine and that its huge Cancer Unit for Children has world renown.

No-one could be prouder of James than his father Cyril, who had always encouraged and supported him. The one regret that Cyril had was that Muriel, his beloved wife, had not lived long enough to see her eldest son's achievement. James had girlfriends but he never married. He chose to dedicate his life to his work and have no distractions. His father, siblings and their families were enough for him. He loved all the time he spent with them and was a favourite uncle of his nephews and nieces

# Chapter 14

When Eleanor told Cyril on the day that he went there for tea, that Benjamin and Victoria had invited him to go and stay with them in the Lake District for a short while to meet his new grandson, Cyril decided almost at once that he would take up the invitation, and the thought entered his mind that the invitation had come at a very opportune moment because he could truthfully tell Doris, if and when he saw her again, that he was going away and would not be visiting her in the near future. He was in his seventies now and in good health and he did not want anyone spoiling the life he enjoyed so much. He was surprised even to think this without Muriel at his side, but it was true. His family were looking after him and he delighted in his grandchildren, the third of whom was only a few weeks old. He had always been of the opinion that each day was a gift to be used in the best possible way or to put it another way "Today is the first day of the rest of your life" and was not to be wasted. Life is for living was this philosophy and that had helped him as he had slowly recovered from Muriel's death.

Eleanor and he started to plan his journey to the Lake District. The 'Railway Age' of the 19th century had been revolutionary to travel. The speed in which one could get to another place by train was phenomenal and the large network of railway lines which criss-crossed the country meant that people could travel by train to almost any part of the country. There was a train to Carlisle from the Central Station, but when he reached Carlisle, he would be taken by horse and carriage to Penrith where he could get a train to Keswick. Benjamin and Victoria would meet him there. Cyril was so excited about what he called his adventure, and it was a very happy Cyril who just one week later waved goodbye to Eleanor, Tom, Elizabeth, Jack and Annabel, to embark on the first stage of his journey. He had felt slightly disturbed since his last meeting with Doris and all the questions she had asked, and this trip to see his grandson was just what he needed.

He sat back in his seat to enjoy the journey. It was a novel experience travelling by train and he was fascinated as the landscape flashed past at such speed. His son Frank was a railway engineer and he had talked endlessly to his father about the beginning of railways. The building of locomotives and steam engines had their origins in the North East, and Frank had made sure that his father was familiar with the two great railway engineers of the century, George Stephenson and his son Robert. Frank's enthusiasm was infectious, and Cyril marvelled as did his son at the ingenuity of these two great men who were both born only a few miles out of Newcastle. Amazingly, George Stephenson was illiterate for most of his life, but he had a marvellous aptitude for anything mechanical, and was constantly being called out when problems arose with engines, or any other engineering works. He could always solve the problem. George had no formal education, but he made sure that his only son Robert was educated. Together they made history and the North East of England is justly very proud of them. One of Cyril's favourite things to do was go down to the River Tyne and walk across the High-Level Bridge and every time he did that he marvelled at its structure. The bridge was very necessary at the time it was built because with the coming of Railways a bridge was needed to carry trains across the River Tyne. The contract for designing such a bridge was given to Robert Stephenson who produced a two-tier structure with three railway tracks on the upper deck and a road below it. Work started on the bridge in 1846 and was completed in June 1849. In August of that year the first passenger train crossed the new High-Level Bridge. It was officially opened by Queen Victoria on September 28th 1849. The roadway beneath the rail deck was opened in February 1850.

As more and more train journeys were being made towards the end of the 19th century it became clear that the High-Level Bridge could not cope with all the rail traffic that passed over it each day and it was obvious that another railway bridge was needed. Work was started on what would be the King Edward VIIth Bridge in July 1902 and it was opened by King Edward VIIth in July 1906.

Thinking of his son Frank who had worked so hard to be where he was today, a Railway Engineer, Cyril was glad that he had been able to educate all his children very well. Education was vital to learning and achieving and building confidence, although not everybody shared that view in the middle of the 19th century. Earning enough money to live was a priority for many people, especially those living in the poorer areas of Newcastle. He was fortunate to be in his present position in that he could afford to send his children to a good school. He had supported them in their different paths of study after giving them the freedom to choose what that study would be. He was very thankful that each of his children were happy with their choice of career. Again, he felt sad to think that Muriel had not lived to see the happiness and success of their children and more importantly could not share it with them.

All their children had attended Dame Allan's School because Cyril liked the ethos of the school. The school was founded by Dame Eleanor Allan in 1705. She was the daughter of a local city goldsmith and married a wealthy tobacco merchant. She lived in Newcastle with her husband and son Francis. Her husband had a tobacco shop in Newcastle, but he was not a good businessman and lost so much of his wealth that when he died Dame Allan and her son Francis were in debt. They took over the tobacco business and made it a considerable success. They then bought a farm in Wallsend in 1700, Wallsend being on the outskirts of Newcastle, and together made a success of running a farm. Sadly, Francis, who was unmarried, died before his mother and she decided to use the money from the tenants of the farm to establish and run a school administered by a Board of Trustees, for 40 poor boys and 20 poor girls from the parishes of St. Nicholas and St. John. These were two of the four prominent parish churches in Newcastle at that time.

It was sad that Dame Allan died the year after her school opened near St. Nicholas's Cathedral. The school moved to different sites in Newcastle over the years until it settled in College Street in Newcastle where it stayed from 1883 to 1935. In this building the boys were on the first floor and the girls on the ground floor. Co-education did not exist. When James, Frank, and Harry had attended the school it was sited at Rosemary Lane in the West End of Newcastle, but it had moved to Hanover Square in 1875 when Benjamin and Eleanor attended. (The school would move later in 1935 to its present home in Fenham.) Cyril had never regretted sending his children to that school because he believed in its theory that the moral, social and spiritual development of pupils was as important as academic success. He wanted his children to grow up to be good citizens and this school would certainly encourage and promote good citizenship.

Cyril was very reflective as the train sped along and as often happened when he was alone, his thoughts turned to Muriel. She would have loved this journey he was making now. Even now he shuddered when he thought about her death, because he should have been able to help her. She had had asthma attacks before although admittedly not nearly a severe as the one that killed her, and he had always managed to help her on other occasions but the asthma attack that killed her was very severe indeed and he was unable to save her. It was a terrible death, and he would always live with the guilt of not being able to save her. It was still, of course, a mystery as to what had caused such a severe attack considering she had not had even a mild attack for years. Something must have brought it on, but Muriel had died before she could tell him and so he would never know. Someone surely must know and back came that feeling that there was something he was not being told.

Thinking back to Eleanor's wedding, he remembered how suddenly Muriel had sat down and turned white as if she was faint and when he helped her to her feet again, she had gripped his hand very tightly as if she was scared of something and yet she said nothing about it. Even when he and Muriel went to bed that night, she had not said anything but snuggled down in a way she had not done for some time. She used to do that if she had to confess to something she had done, such as spending too much money on one of her numerous shopping trips. She never needed to worry because he loved her so much that she could do no wrong in his eyes.

Cyril could hardly believe it when the train reached Carlisle. It had taken such a short time. What a difference this new form of transport made. From Carlisle his journey to Penrith was much slower as he had to travel by horse and carriage, but he enjoyed the journey nonetheless. The train from Penrith took him to Keswick and he saw Benjamin and Victoria with their baby son waiting for him on the platform. They gave him a huge welcome and after admiring and greeting his new grandson the family set off to enjoy what was to be a very happy time for Cyril. Spending time with his family were the happiest times in Cyril's life. They were also the times when he missed Muriel the most, but he must put all those thoughts away now and just enjoy the days ahead with his new grandson. The weather being late Spring was favourable and everyday Cyril, Victoria and Benjamin took advantage of it and had some lovely walks, proudly pushing Edward in his pram. Their cottage was within sight of Lake Derwentwater and their favourite walk was to Friar's Crag on the Lake's edge, from where they could look up the lake to the valley of Borrowdale. It was a beautiful place at which to stand and take in the beauty and grandeur of the mountains and the gentle rippling water of the lake. This was beauty which must never be allowed to be spoilt. Cyril wondered how many other people had stood on Friar's Crag enjoying the beauty around them. Reader, we could tell him today that it is still a very well-loved, popular place to stand and admire the view and that there is a special memorial there. It is to the memory of John Ruskin, one of the greatest figures of the Victorian Age. He was born in 1819 and died in 1900. He led a distinguished life as a writer, a poet, an artist, a social reformer, a conservationist and above all the most influential art critic of nineteenth century Britain. He bought a property called Brantwood on Lake Coniston in 1861 and lived there in his retirement from 1885 to his death in 1900.

The words on the John Ruskin Memorial read:

'The first thing that I remember as an event in my life was being taken by my nurse to the brow of Friar's Crag on Derwentwater.'

That first view of Friar's Crag made a deep impression on the 5-year-old boy and years later he described the incident as "the creation of the world for me".

John Ruskin would have been in complete agreement with Cyril who was very glad that in 1904 something was done to protect areas of outstanding beauty in England,

Scotland and Wales and never allow them to be neglected. This was the beginning of 'The National Trust' which came into being because at the end of the 19th century, three visionary people planned to care for nature, beauty and history at a National Level. The three people were Octavia Hill, Sir Robert Hunter and Canon Hardwicke Rawnsley and they were the founders of The National Trust which was formally constituted on 12th January 1895

Octavia Hill was born in 1838 and was a pioneer in housing improvements and in the defence of open spaces against urban encroachment. She was the eighth daughter of a banker.

Sir Robert Hunter was born in 1844 and was a solicitor, who from the 1860s was very interested in the conservation of public open spaces. It was he who came up with the idea for the organisation and paved the way for its legal creation. He served as the first Chairman.

Canon Hardwicke Drummond Rawnsley was an Anglican Priest, a poet, a local politician and a conservationist. He became nationally and internationally known as one of the three founders of the National Trust. He was born in 1851 and died at Grasmere in 1920. He was vicar of Crosthwaite Church in Keswick from 1883-1917 and was a great lover of the Lake District. He was a good friend of the celebrated writer and illustrator Beatrix Potter, who fully supported the efforts of the National Trust and being a conservationist was interested in building up breeds of animals. She actually became famous for breeding Herdwick sheep.

Cyril would not have described himself as a religious man, but in the midst of such beauty and majesty which epitomised the Lake District, he could believe in a Creator God. He had read Genesis, the first chapter of Genesis at the beginning of the family Bible that he had shown Annabel one day. It was all about the creation of the world and although he had difficulty with the concept of the world being made in seven days, he had to believe that the beauty of creation could not have come about through an ordinary human being. The first verse of the Bible reads 'In the beginning God' and he believed there had to be a beginning for the world and he could definitely believe it was God. Had he been able to read the words on the back of the above-mentioned Ruskin memorial I think he would have agreed with them.

'The Spirit of God is around you in the air that you breathe.

His Glory in the Light that you see,

And in the fruitfulness of the earth and the joy of its creatures

He has written for you day by day

His revelation, as he has granted you Day by Day your Daily Bread.'

# Chapter 15

C yril thoroughly enjoyed his short stay in the Lake District and was very sorry when it was time to return home. Benjamin and Victoria were sorry too and certainly baby Edward would miss all the attention his grandfather had given him, but as Benjamin said, 'All good things come to an end'. The visit had helped to take his mind off the things that were bothering him and now he was looking forward to seeing Tom, Eleanor and the children again. They were all waiting for him at the Central Station and there were lots of hugs and kisses, though Cyril did not think Annabel looked like her usual happy self. She looked pre-occupied about something.

He asked her if anything was the matter, but she shook her head. The next day he decided to meet Annabel off the horse drawn carriage vehicle which took her to school each day. He knew the time it arrived at Summerhill and was waiting for her there. The Transport System had been modernised in 1901 by Newcastle Public Transport and Newcastle Corporation Tramways; electric trams were introduced to Newcastle city streets but trams did not come up the West Road.

'Annabel, where is your lovely smile today?' He was surprised when she burst into tears. It did not take long for her to tell him why she was so upset.

'Grandpa, it is all happening again. I just could not believe it when someone in my class at St Paul's School turned up in my new school. Her parents have split up and she is living with her grandma in the centre of Newcastle near Dame Allan's School. Her grandparents have sent her to my school but that would not matter except that her first words to me were 'Have they let you out of the Workhouse' and so, Grandpa, it is all happening again. Every time I pass her at school, she says, 'Hi workhouse girl' and the girls with her snigger and laugh. I hate it and I want Mummy and Daddy to take me away from that school, but they won't, I know they won't and I hate them, and I hate everyone except you, Grandpa, because I know you will help me.'

'Yes, I will Annabel, but I will have to have a good think about it. Now try to forget about it tonight, have a good sleep You do not have to go to school tomorrow because it is Saturday and I will have thought of something to do about your problem by the time Monday comes so do not worry anymore.'

Cyril felt so sorry for her. He hated to see a child as miserable as that, but he was not at all sure what he was going to do.

The very next morning he was awakened by a distraught Ella knocking loudly on his door. 'Annabel has gone,' she cried. 'Her bedclothes and pyjamas were thrown across the bed when I went into her room this morning. Her school uniform is still on the bedside chair but some of her clothes have gone from the drawers and wardrobe so she must have dressed herself. She has not taken anything else with her and her little leather money purse is still there, but she has obviously run away. She seemed upset when she came home from school last night but would not tell me about it and when I went up to her bedroom later in the evening to say goodnight, she was sobbing but again would not confide in me. What are we going to do?'

'Calm down, Ella,' Cyril said reassuringly 'she will not have gone far because you say she has not taken anything with her, and her little money purse is still beside her bed. We will find her but first we will go round to Eleanor's house to tell her what has happened.'

Eleanor was shocked to hear what had happened and said that after she had dressed the children and given them breakfast, they would come and join the search.

Ella, Phillip, and Cyril set off immediately to look for Annabel but all to no avail. They asked people if they had seen a young girl about eleven years old, wandering around by herself, after describing Annabel to them but no-one had seen her. Cyril said when they all met up again that they would have to tell the police though they were very reluctant to do that. Ella's parents were very hesitant to tell anyone that their daughter had run away and so the search went on all afternoon, but Annabel was nowhere to be found and as darkness began to fall, Ella and Phillip knew they would have to tell the police. It was so frightening because the police asked a lot of questions as well as being reassuring in saying that if their little girl had run away, they would find her and that in their experience these children usually returned home the same day. Unfortunately, after searching all day for her, Annabel did not return home and they had another sleepless night. Everyone was trying to think of a reason why Annabel would run away until Cyril gave them a clue saying Annabel had told him that she was very unhappy at school. He had to tell them that she was being called names again by a girl who had attended St Paul's School when she was there and the nasty names they called her included the word which upset her the most, workhouse. Ella and Phillip knew nothing of all this and were very upset that they had not been told. Annabel had said nothing to them. Cyril explained that Annabel had told him that she loved them so much she did not want to worry them and in his opinion she had run away so as not to cause them any more worry. What she had done, of course, was made the situation much worse. Her parents were desperately worried about her.

Annabel had waited until her parents had gone to bed then changed out of her pyjamas into trousers and a top and a cardigan in case it was cold during the night and very, very quietly, she had crept downstairs, opened the back door and run as fast as she could away from the house.

She was running so fast with her head bent low that she did not see the person coming towards her and bumped right into them. The woman took her by the shoulders and bent down to look at her.

'Annabel Gibson, I do believe. Wherever are you going at this time of the morning?' Doris Swift exclaimed. She was on her way home at two o'clock in the morning from a night at the pub with her friends and was a little tipsy.

Annabel recognised the voice as being that cleaner lady from St Paul's School.

'I am running away because I do not want to go back to my new school,' Annabel replied.

'Why ever not, Annabel, you are a clever, very pretty little girl.'

'Nasty people are calling me names again, just like they did at St Paul's School that is why and I had enough of that at St Paul's School.'

'Then it is lucky that I have found you, Annabel. I am just the right person to help you. Fancy anyone being nasty to you and shouting nasty names. That is a shocking thing to do. Now stop those tears which are rolling down your face. I know your Grandpa very well and I will tell him where you are because he will be worried about you, but first, I will take you home with me and give you a drink and something to eat until you feel better.' At last, Doris thought to herself, I have the chance to make Cyril suffer.

Doris took Annabel's hand and led her to her house. Annabel was by now realising that she had been silly and was so glad that she would soon be reunited with her family. She was not to know that Doris was not her friend and had no intention of returning Annabel to her family just yet. It was the chance she had been waiting for to get revenge on Cyril. He would be sorry for dismissing her so easily and playing with her affections. How dare he reject her! Kidnapping

Annabel had come at a very opportune time because none of her three children were at home. Their worthless father had actually taken the children away on holiday. Perhaps he was not so worthless after all because his timing could not have been better. Had the children been at home it would have been difficult to explain Annabel's sudden appearance in their home. Her husband had unexpectedly won some money in a competition and wonder of wonders had decided to give the children, whom he seldom saw or even thought about, a special treat. Doris had been furious to find out that she was not included in his magnanimous gesture, but now she could not be better pleased. Here was her chance to punish Cyril. After something to eat and drink she had settled Annabel down in her daughter's bed and told her to have as long a sleep as she wanted. It was Saturday tomorrow. She did not need to worry about home because she would take her home tomorrow when she woke up. As soon as Annabel was asleep, Doris sat down to plan what she was going to do next.

Meanwhile the search for Annabel continued but she could not be found. Cyril was absolutely exhausted by the next evening and Eleanor was getting quite worried about him. He said he was getting pains in his chest and she was afraid that he was going to have a heart attack. She made him go to bed to rest but he could not rest because he was worrying so much about Annabel. He should have gone to see the headteacher straight away and begged her to stop the children being so unkind to Annabel. He should also have told her parents much more about it though they must have noticed that Annabel was very unhappy. He tortured himself with these thoughts, longing to hear her voice again. He loved that little girl with all his heart. The next morning Cyril decided to go to Doris's house and see if she had seen Annabel. The police arrived just after he got back and wanted to know where he had been.

'It came to me through the night that Doris who knew Annabel from St Paul's School might be able to help me,' Cyril said.

'We will make that our first call,' the policeman said, 'because we know that family very well.'

Meanwhile Doris was very pleased with herself when she got up on Saturday morning. She actually saw Cyril looking very worried passing her window and obviously looking for something or someone. He was closely followed by Eleanor looking equally worried. Doris smiled to herself. They were obviously suffering and that was what she wanted. When he had suffered enough, she would tell him that she had taken his daughter Annabel, yes, his daughter and she would tell him the truth about his precious wife. Muriel was not the woman he thought she was, and she wanted to see his shocked face. It was all his fault. If he had shown interest in a relationship with her this would not have happened.

When Annabel awoke on Saturday morning, she was confused by her surroundings. This was not her home. Where was she? Then she remembered she had run away and that kind lady who worked as a cleaner at her old school had found her and taken her into her home. She got up and went to find her.

'Are you going to take me back to my mummy now?' she asked.

'I will give you some breakfast and then we will go back to your house,' Doris replied, but she had other plans.

'I will take you back, Annabel, but I thought we would go to the workhouse first because I have to return something.'

'Workhouse,' Annabel said. 'That is what horrible children at my school keep shouting at me. I would like to see what a workhouse is but first I really want to see my mammy and daddy. They will be so worried.' Annabel could feel tears beginning behind her eyes.

'Go upstairs and wash your face and hands first, and then I will take you to them,' Doris said.

What happened next was fortunate for Annabel but unfortunate for Doris. Annabel quickly ran upstairs to wash her face and even more quickly ran down the stairs, but her foot caught on what was a rather large hole in the carpet and she fell down the rest of the stairs, hitting her head on the umbrella stand at the bottom of the stairs. It really hurt and she screamed. Doris ran to her and lifted her up but when Annabel put her foot to the floor she screamed again with the pain in her ankle. Doris had certainly not planned for this to happen. The little girl could not walk on her foot and had obviously damaged it. She dared not go for help. because all her neighbours knew that her three children had gone away with their father. They all knew about it because Doris had told them what she thought of their father, this being the only time he had shown any interest in his children since he left home. One thing was certain, they must not see Annabel. She lifted Annabel up and somehow, although she was heavy, Doris carried her upstairs and lay her on the bed. A big lump had started to come up on Annabel's forehead and she brought a wet cloth to put over it. Annabel would not stop crying. Over and over again she said that she wanted her mummy and tears were pouring down her cheeks. Doris, for the very first time, wished that she had not taken Annabel into her house. She did not know what she was going to do next. She could not do anything until it was dark because she could not risk anyone seeing her leave Doris's house. Fortunately, Annabel was so tired with all her sobbing that she had fallen asleep again and when she woke up in the early hours of the morning, Doris said she would make her something to eat and then when it was light she would take her home. Somehow Doris managed to get through the night but because Annabel was so sleepy, she was terrified that the head wound she had sustained after falling down the stairs was more serious. Annabel's ankle was swelling and needed attention and Doris spent a very long, worrying night, wondering what she should do the next day.

It was taken out of her hands when the next morning there was loud knocking on her front door. She ran downstairs to open it only to find Cyril standing there.

'Doris,' Cyril said breathlessly because he had run up the hill to her house. 'Have you by any chance seen Annabel? She ran away from home through the night on Friday and we have not seen her since. We are all frantic with worry.'

'So sorry, Cyril. I have not seen her. What a dreadful thing to happen. Do you think she could have walked up to the workhouse? She might have been curious about it because of the children shouting that word at her. I would try there.'

'You seem to know a lot about the name calling, Doris,' Cyril said. 'I do hope you had nothing to do with it, I thought you were a friend. We have told the police about it and they are going to help us today. It is looking more and more as if someone has taken her away.'

Doris was regretting what she had done when she heard the word Police. She had been in trouble before with them and had been let off with a warning, but if she was caught again doing something wrong, she would be in big trouble.

She had to get rid of Cyril, and so she said she would help with the search if she could because she knew what Annabel looked like.

Cyril said again, 'You seem to know a lot about Annabel, Doris. When I talked about her at your house you did not mention that you knew her very well, which is strange.'

Doris was glad when Cyril left, and she went to check on Annabel who was still sleeping, but when she drew back the bed clothes, she saw that Annabel's ankle was badly swollen and a funny shape. She realised the ankle was broken and that, somehow, she would have to get her to hospital for doctors to see it.

Oh dear. This had certainly not been part of the plan. There was another loud knock on the front door and Doris was shocked to find a policeman on her doorstep.

He explained that he was looking for a ten-year-old girl who was missing from home. Doris made a great show of saying how much she would have liked to help but she had never seen anyone in the last two days because she had been in bed nursing a cold. Just after speaking there was a piercing scream from somewhere in the house and the police officer pushed Doris to the side and went into the house, despite loud protests from Doris. They had recognised Doris and knew she was not trustworthy. Her oldest son was a bully and often got into trouble with the police, so it was necessary to check this family out. At the top of the stairs stood Annabel screaming and shouting for her mummy at the top of her voice. She was extremely agitated.

'My leg hurts, my leg hurts,' she sobbed, 'I cannot walk, I cannot walk.'

The police officer lifted her up and carried her downstairs. It was fortunate that there was another officer outside and he handed the little girl to him, urging him to contact the parents as quickly as he could. He then took charge of Doris and warned her that she was being arrested for kidnapping and concealing a child who was not her own. He warned her that she had committed an offence and must be very careful in what she said as that could lead to further trouble for her. By now Doris knew that she had been very foolish, and she was afraid of the consequences of her behaviour. As she was taken away in the police car he was sure there would be prying eyes behind the windows of the houses near her and she would have a lot of explaining to do.

The relief when Annabel was safely home again was immense for the family. It was necessary to take her straight to the hospital to see about her broken ankle and it took some time for the family to settle down again. Cyril was furious at what Doris had done, especially when he realised that she was behind all the name calling and misery that Annabel had endured. She deserved any punishment she was given, and he would make sure that she never came near

Annabel again. He still did not understand why Doris was so interested in Annabel and why she had targeted her for her unkind taunts, but he was determined now to find out.

Eleanor was extremely worried about what had happened and was terrified that the police might ask Doris questions that could incriminate her late mother The secret which she had kept for so long might not remain a secret and she feared greatly for her family Over the following weeks she felt the weight of her secret terribly and had to watch her father getting more and more distressed because he blamed himself for not doing more to help Annabel's worries at her new school He should have watched over Annabel more carefully

# Chapter 16

C yril was very unhappy, and Eleanor thought it would be a good idea for him to go away again to the Lake District. It was fortuitous that Harry, Kate and Frank were about to go to there because at last they had been able to arrange a date for their climb of Helvellyn. James was going to join them at Glenridding beside Lake Ullswater and go home the next day, so that he took as little time off work as he could. Harry and Kate and Frank were quite happy to take their father with them to Ben and Victoria's home. Eleanor arranged everything for Cyril, and he joined Frank, Harry and Kate at the Central Station for the journey to the Lake District. He immediately felt better when he saw the mountains and green fields and was delighted to see Edward, his grandson once again. He was growing fast and already pulling himself up around the furniture. He was a delightful little boy.

James, Harry and Frank were very excited about the climb. It presented a great challenge for them because the route they were taking was the most difficult one. Climbing Helvellyn this way meant they had to walk along 'Striding Edge'. The latter was very precarious and dangerous, and people had lost their lives crossing it but that did not deter the brothers. It made them more eager and determined to climb it. Harry had brought Kate with him to stay and keep Victoria company while the brothers were away. Victoria was really looking forward to seeing Kate again. She had not met baby Edward yet and Victoria would enjoy showing him off to her friend. He was now nine months old and Kate thought he was a lovely baby and Victoria talked enthusiastically about how much she was enjoying motherhood. She knew Kate would want to push the pram and she had planned some lovely walks for them in and around Keswick.

It was a full house at Benjamin and Victoria's cottage, but it was great fun. Plans were being made for the brothers' big climb. They had to get to Glenridding on the shores of Lake Ullswater in order to meet James and begin the climb. Glenridding was a half hour journey away and a horse and carriage was going to take them there. They waved excitedly to Cyril, Ben, Victoria and Kate They were going to stay overnight in Glenridding after the climb and then make an early start for home. Harry, Kate and Frank were going to stay on for another week at Ben's house.

Climbing Helvellyn, England's third highest mountain, was going to be a challenge, but Harry had made himself the leader and he constantly encouraged his brothers. He had to do a lot of persuading when they reached 'Striding

Edge' because Frank and James wanted to drop out of the climb. 'Striding Edge' is a slender winding track along the top of a steep ridge that leads to the summit of Helvellyn. In places it is less than three feet wide with an awesome drop on either side. On a good day it is relatively safe but in bad weather it is a perilous place. The day was dull and dry underfoot, but Frank and James were very reluctant to go further. Harry cajoled and almost begged them to continue, which eventually they did and agreed when they reached the summit of the mountain with its magnificent views that it had all been worth it, not of course knowing what was going to happen.

Harry and Frank away climbing meant that Cyril, Kate, Ben, Victoria and baby Edward had a lovely long day to do something themselves. Victoria and Kate were happy to take Edward out in his pram to have one of the walks that Victoria had planned, and they would be able to enjoy catching up with one another's lives. Kate told Victoria excitedly that Harry had proposed to her at last and they were to be married during the next year. Needless to say, Victoria was delighted for Kate and was very happy to talk about weddings with her.

Ben had done some thinking about his father's second visit and had decided they would visit Sawrey in West Cumbria. He had read in the local paper about a lady called Beatrix Potter, who had a great love of art and had moved to the Lake District, after her fiancé died in 1905. She was reputed to be a very talented artist and Benjamin wanted to know more about her. He already knew about her great love of the countryside and the Lake District, where she had spent many holidays with her parents when she was young. While there she spent as much time as she could, exploring and sketching the animals and flowers she discovered.

She was born in London on the 28th of July in 1866 into a wealthy middle-class family. Her father was an artist and Beatrix learned a great deal about painting techniques from him. By the age of eight she was filling sketch books with drawings of animals and plants copied from nature or any books she could find on the subject. She had drawing lessons and attended the National Art Training School in London between 1878 and 1883. In her twenties she made studies of plants and animals at the Natural History Museum and learned how to draw what she saw under a microscope. In 1890 she got her first illustration commission from a greeting card company and was very thrilled. Her children's books evolved from illustrated letters which she used to send to her former governess's children. The first of these books was to Noel in 1893 and it featured a rabbit. This book was called 'The Tale of Peter Rabbit' and was published in 1902. It was a great success and an article about this talented lady had appeared in the press and was the source of Benjamin's knowledge about her. He was not to know then that 'Peter Rabbit' was only the first of many other books she wrote featuring animals.

Benjamin had managed to get a copy of the first book 'Peter Rabbit' and it had fired his imagination and strengthened his ambition to one day have his own little shop and sell some of his paintings and crafts. Meantime, visiting the area where Beatrix lived would be inspiring for him and he was looking forward to a really good day with his father.

They had never been particularly close when Benjamin was young, but were certainly developing a closeness as he got older. Cyril was much more appreciative of the work his son did. He was sure that one day his son would have an exhibition of his paintings. He was very talented.

Cyril and Benjamin thoroughly enjoyed the time they spent at Sawrey. Benjamin had hired a horse and trap for the journey which made the latter very pleasant as they could admire in their own time the beautiful landscape of hills, and fields and waysides. Sometimes they stopped so that Benjamin could do some sketching and Cyril could sit and admire the surroundings. At Sawrey, they were able to talk to local people when they had lunch in the nearby pub which was a very old building and so cosy with its huge blazing fire and old wooden seating. The people they talked to spoke very kindly of the new lady from London, whom it seemed wanted to learn more about farming, though they had also heard that in London she had been engaged to a man called Norman Warne who had died a month before they were to be married and this had contributed to her move to Sawrey and 'Hill Top' farm. They also knew that she was a writer and that her first book, 'Peter Rabbit' was published in 1902 and was very popular. What they did not know then was that 'Peter Rabbit' would become one of the best loved and bestselling children's books of all time. It was the royalties from 'Peter Rabbit' that had made it possible to buy 'Hill Top' in 1905 which was why, when Benjamin and Cyril visited Sawrey in 1905, Beatrix Potter was living in 'Hill Top', a small 17th century farmhouse on a hill above the western shore of Windermere. She used it as her place to write when she wanted to escape London and many of her characters were conceived there, e.g. Tom Kitten, Samuel Whiskers and Jemima Puddleduck. The local people could not know then that royalties from her writing success allowed her to buy Castle Farm in 1909 which was across the road from Hill Top, and that in 1913 she married William Heelis, a solicitor from Hawkshead who had helped her with her property buying. They kept Castle Farm as their home and Hill Top as a writing retreat for Beatrix.

There was more to add to her story which could not be known then, as she became an astute businesswoman who had a passion for the Lake District and developed a great interest in conservation. It was her intent to preserve the beauty of the Lake District's unique landscape and traditional farming methods and it is no surprise to learn that she had taken up her friendship again with Canon Hardwicke Rawnsley whom she had known since childhood when she holidayed with her parents in the Lake District. She took great interest in his work for the National Trust, preserving places of beauty and protecting the landscape, in addition to preserving traditional farming methods. In 1923 she bought a sheep farm in Troutbeck on the edge of the Lake District and became an expert Herdwick Sheep Breeder, the latter being a small hardy breed of sheep indigenous to the Lake District.

During all this time she was still drawing, painting and writing until her eyesight began to fail. The 'Tale of Little Pig Robinson' was her last major work and this was published in 1930. She continued her work of conservation and preservation in the Lake District until her death in 1943 and left 4,000 acres of the Lake District, 14 farms and all her flocks of Herdwick sheep to the National Trust. It was a great legacy from a great person who will always be held in very high regard.

Benjamin and Cyril had had a lovely day and there was a lot of conversation during their evening meal. Beatrix Potter featured a great deal in the table talk and Benjamin enthused so much about Beatrix and how she was already endearing herself to the local people that Victoria said he must take her there so that she could perhaps see this very talented lady who not only wrote the books but also illustrated them so beautifully. They would take Edward with them because he would enjoy such an outing, riding in a horse and cart and seeing all the animals in the fields.

It was late evening when Cyril, Benjamin, Victoria and Kate sat down to their evening meal. Edward had found his day too exciting to fall asleep in his pram as he usually did and so was very tired. Victoria had been able to get him to bed and asleep before the evening meal and so there was uninterrupted time to talk about their day and they all wondered how the boys had got on climbing Helvellyn. They would hear all about it tomorrow. No doubt they were feeling very tired and had probably gone to bed early. It was therefore quite a surprise to be woken up in the early hours of the morning by Harry banging on the front door and even more of a surprise to see that he was accompanied by a police officer.

Harry's voice was shaking as he said, 'Dad, Frank has had an accident and is in hospital at Carlisle and the Police have brought me here so that we can take you back there.'

There was such a sense of urgency in his voice that Cyril was already pulling on his clothes as he hurried to the front door. Ben also dressed quickly and mounted the horse drawn carriage, which was the police transport at that time. Once in the carriage Cyril asked Harry to tell him what had happened, and he also wanted to know the whereabouts of James.

Harry explained that James was sitting beside Frank's bed in the hospital.

'Then obviously it is serious,' Cyril said. 'Tell me what happened.'

'We were walking along 'Striding Edge' when Frank slipped. We tried to hang onto him, but we were not strong enough and Frank fell all the way to the bottom of the cliff. We walked back into Glenridding and went to the police station to get help. They knew immediately who to contact for mountain rescue and they acted very quickly. We were able to tell them exactly where Frank was, and on arriving at the scene they assessed Frank's condition and immediately took him to Carlisle, the nearest major hospital.

'It was horrible seeing Frank lying so still and unconscious, Father and we could see one of his legs was bent right back at a very strange angle and was obviously very badly damaged. We sat waiting for a long time until the doctor came out to tell us that Frank had a very serious head wound and he advised us to tell our family because Frank was gravely ill. His injury was life threatening and he was being taken into the operating theatre for an operation to relieve the pressure on his brain. Frank's leg was also very badly damaged and would need an operation. It was obvious to us that Frank would have to stay in hospital for some time.' Harry tried to keep his composure as he told his father about the accident, but he burst into tears at the end of it. 'It is all my fault,' he sobbed.

When Cyril and Benjamin reached the hospital, they were unable to talk to Frank because he was in an induced coma, and Cyril and Harry had to leave him there while they returned to Benjamin's house. James, however, being a doctor knew just how seriously ill his brother was and he would not leave his side. He would have done anything to help Frank but was very afraid that there was nothing anyone could do to save his brother. He would respect his father's wishes and see if Frank could be transferred to Newcastle, but he lost all hope of this happening because Frank was too ill. The next few days were critical but at one point the doctors thought his condition was improving and Cyril decided to go home to Newcastle so that he would be there when Frank was transferred.

He also decided to visit Muriel's sister Izzy, on the way home because she lived in Carlisle and was the sister whom Muriel had gone to see a few years ago to help her look after her daughter's new baby. She had not been able to come to Muriel's funeral because she was ill. It would be good to see her again. It would help him to talk about other things when he was so worried about his son.

Izzy was delighted to see him and welcomed him warmly. She had always admired Cyril and thought Muriel was very lucky to have such a good husband. It had been a great shock for her when her sister died, and she had regretted not being able to go to the funeral because of illness.

CHAPTER 16

'You will be tired, Cyril, with all the emotional strain of
Frank's accident,' Izzy said. 'I will make you something to
eat and prepare your bed and then you must go there and
have a good sleep. I am looking forward to hearing all about
your family tomorrow, especially the little one. She will be
a young lady now. It is 11 years since I last saw my sister.
How quickly the years pass. What did you call her?' Izzy
continued. 'Does she have Muriel's fabulous blonde curly
hair and big blue eyes? Has she inherited Muriel's beautiful
singing voice? There is so much to talk about, and we can
do that in the morning. Now, have a little rest while I make
some supper and then you are going to bed.'

Cyril closed his eyes but could not go to sleep because he
was very puzzled by Izzy's questions. Whatever did she mean
about his little one? Eleanor was his youngest and she was
now in her late twenties. She had not inherited her mother's
ash blonde curly hair or her mother's beautiful singing
voice. He was still thinking about it when Izzy brought in
the supper and because he was too tired to talk too much
there was no serious conversation. That would come the
next day but for the second time in a few days Cyril was
awakened through the night with a loud knocking on the
door and once again a policeman stood there, and a horse
drawn police carriage was waiting. Cyril felt instinctively
that something was dreadfully wrong, and he was right.
The police were taking him back to the hospital in Carlisle
because his son Frank's condition had worsened, and he was
gravely ill. Cyril could not believe this was happening again
and he found himself praying on the journey to the hospital,
that his son would not die. The journey to the hospital was

99

interminable but he did reach the hospital in time to whisper to his dying son that he loved him very much indeed. He held his son's hand as he died, but then collapsed into a chair and sobbed uncontrollably.

The doctors spoke to Cyril and told him that unfortunately because of Frank's broken leg a clot had formed, which had travelled through his heart to his lungs and this had proved fatal. They were unable to do anything to save him and were very sorry. Frank's death had brought back all the anguish of Muriel's death and Cyril found it difficult to function. He had five children, but he could not spare one of them. He was approaching 70 and it would have made more sense for him to die in place of Frank. The whole family, of course, were devastated at Frank's death and Cyril, who had gone back to Ben and Victoria's house when he left the hospital, sat all day long not speaking a word and not even looking at them. He was in a state of shock. They had thought that his grandson Edward would raise a smile from him but even that was too much for Cyril. His son's death was as sudden and tragic as Muriel's, and the loss of two dearly loved members of his family was too much to bear.

James and Harry dealt with all the business and made sure Frank's body was going to be taken back to Newcastle. Cyril wanted his son buried next to his mother in St. Paul's churchyard, on the West Road near Summerhill where they lived.

Eleanor went to Keswick and brought Cyril back to Newcastle and took him into her home to stay until the shock of Frank's death had worn off a little. She also thought Elizabeth and Jack would help her father's recovery, but he did not want to be near anyone, and Eleanor became afraid that he was sinking into depression. James and Harry looked in when they were able and the ever lively Annabel skipped in one evening after school.

'Now come on, Grandpa, we need you and you have got to get better. I want you to help me to make up my mind about what I want to do when I leave school. I am sure Uncle Frank would not want you to be so miserable. When I come tomorrow night, I want you to have a smile.'

Cyril never could resist the charms of Annabel and he promised he would try. Slowly but surely, Cyril began to feel better. In the early days after Frank died, he had thought about Frank from getting up in the morning to going to bed at night, but gradually he could think about his son without getting too upset. Cyril had always enjoyed Frank's company and together they had discussed 'The Railway Age' which was so much part of the Victorian Era. It had revolutionised transport and Frank who had always been interested in trains from being a small boy and who became a Railway Engineer, could talk very knowledgably about locomotives, steam engines, and the vast network of railway lines that were being laid. This had led to railway stations being built in certain parts of the country and Newcastle was very proud of their Central Station which had been designed by none other than John Dobson, the famous architect whose name was synonymous with Newcastle upon Tyne. Work to build the station had begun in 1845 and it was opened by Queen Victoria and Prince Albert in 1850. It was considered to be of a very grand design. The portico was added to it in 1851.

# Chapter 17

T he introduction of railways had come to Tyneside at just the right time for the coal trade, which was the major industry in the North-East in the 19th century. This was because the coal trade and supplies of coal from local pits around Newcastle and Gateshead were gradually becoming exhausted in the 19th century. Railways, however, allowed more distant collieries to transport coal cheaply and quickly to the River Tyne from where it could be sent to other countries. Railways themselves provided more work for local companies, who were kept busy producing bars, cables and machined parts for engines, railway lines and metal components for bridges. It was the beginning of a surge of economic growth for the country and Frank had often told his father how proud he felt to be a part of something that in his eyes was the greatest innovation of the 19th century. The week before he died, he had been talking enthusiastically about his work as a Railway Engineer which he absolutely loved. Frank had a zest for life which was infectious, and Cyril missed him terribly.

It seemed so unfair that Frank had died before himself, now approaching 70 years of age. He would gladly have taken Frank's place although he knew that no-one is able to choose when and how they die. It was tragic that what had been planned as a happy, adventurous climb had ended in Frank's death. The brothers had planned so carefully and responsibly but that had not been enough to keep Frank safe. Philosophically Cyril knew that life had to go on and he was very fortunate to still have four very caring children. He knew he had to come to terms with his loss, but it was not easy. It would not do him any good to be bitter and no blame could be attached to anyone, although Harry was fretting so much about he himself being to blame because he had suggested using the route over Striding Edge, knowing it was more difficult than other routes. Cyril tried to give him the reassurance that he needed, but it took Harry a long time to forgive himself and he needed a lot of support. He could not bear his father's grief-stricken face at first and was glad when Eleanor came to Keswick to take Cyril home to Newcastle. He and James had to attend to a lot of business matters, not least making sure that Frank's body was taken home to Newcastle, but Harry was happy to be kept busy so that he could not dwell too much on the circumstances of Frank's death.

The following weeks were very difficult for the whole family, and Cyril, who was living with Eleanor at her insistence, was very depressed. Eleanor and Tom were very worried about him. 'We will have to try and get him interested in something,' Eleanor said. Even the children Elizabeth and Jack could not raise his spirits. Annabel made regular visits to Eleanor's home but even she failed to make him smile. Eleanor had always liked walking, especially pushing a pram or pushchair, and whenever she took the children for a walk, she always included her father. It saddened her to see him so downcast and she tried desperately to think of something which could lighten his spirits.

One day Eleanor and Tom took her father with them to the library in town to get out some books for herself and Tom. Their interest in books had never waned and they were still frequent visitors to the library. The latter had special memories for them because it was their love of books which had first brought them together. Eleanor felt that she should have thought to take her father to the library sooner because it was from him that she and her siblings had learnt to love books and appreciate their value. Cyril enjoyed the visit, browsing through the books, but while waiting for Eleanor and Tom he told them that he wanted to look in the building next to the library which was relatively new. It was called the Laing Art Gallery, named after its founder Alexander Laing. Eleanor said they would come and find him there.

The Newcastle Council had been conscious at the beginning of the 20th century, that the now expanding city did not have an art gallery, but it was experiencing difficulty in raising funds to build one. Alexander Laing was a wealthy Scottish businessman who had become rich in the city by establishing his own bottling company before branching out into wines and spirits. It appeared that he wanted to give something back to the city in which he had made his fortune and in 1900 he offered £20,000 to Newcastle Council, to fund the building of an Art Gallery, which of course was gratefully accepted. In 1901, the foundation stone was laid and there was a celebratory lunch at the great Assembly Rooms at the bottom of the West Road, not far from St John's church. The Gallery was huge and took three years to build, costing Alexander Laing 50% more than originally estimated. Cyril, looking at it now, thought it was a magnificent building and then recalled a newspaper item about it when it was opened to the public. There were so many people at the opening that the police had to be brought in to control the crowds.

The building held exhibitions of British paintings, work by local artists and world cultures, all of which were greatly admired. Cyril spent considerable time there walking round the rooms looking at all the artwork exhibited in them. He could not help thinking how much his son Benjamin and his wife Victoria would enjoy this gallery and he resolved to bring them here when they next visited their family in Newcastle. He became so engrossed in the paintings that Eleanor and Tom had to come looking for him and they too found the gallery extremely interesting. They also decided that they must come another day and spend more time there looking round the varied exhibits. They were very pleased to see Cyril looking much more relaxed and he even greeted them with a smile. He had not been smiling very much in recent weeks and was very withdrawn and very unlike his usual self. She felt hopeful that today was a beginning for Cyril to take up his customary interest and positivity for life.

The Gallery became Cyril's favourite place and he visited it regularly in the following weeks. He walked or cycled to the Gallery every day and he seemed to find peace there. He also found the cycling beneficial to his health. In fact, now that he was feeling better, he might join one of the cycling clubs in Newcastle. He had bought his bicycle in 1884 when the new safety bicycle was manufactured. This bicycle had two wheels of the same size driven round by pedals and a chain. The first pedal bicycles had appeared in 1839 and cycling soon became popular, but not all bicycles were safe to ride mainly because of different sized wheels like the 'penny farthing' which came out in 1870.

Cyril became well known as a frequent visitor at the Art Gallery and was actually given a part-time job there as a steward in one of the exhibition rooms. It meant he was in touch with people again and had found a purpose for his day. Life now had a normality about it and sometimes he was able to spend time at the library too, all of which helped him to come to terms with his grief. In July 1906, one whole year after Frank's death, Cyril would be 70 years of age and to his surprise the staff at the Gallery had a special tea party for him in one of their meeting rooms. They had become very fond of this well-mannered, well dressed, well-spoken gentleman who was so interested in art and culture. His friends from the library had also been asked to the party along with Eleanor and Tom, and the former was so proud of her father and so glad to see him happy again. She was glad too that her secret was still intact, because she knew he had visited Muriel's sister in Carlisle where he might have been asked questions about Muriel and her baby. It was obvious that Cyril had not been told too much by Izzy, and Eleanor was very relieved. At the present time he could not have dealt with all the emotion which would inevitably follow if he found out about Muriel's deceit. What Eleanor did not know was that Izzy had asked Cyril a lot of questions, but Cyril had not had the chance to answer them owing to the arrival of the police and his leaving her house to go to the hospital. She would have been very worried if she knew that her father wanted to ask Izzy more questions to which he wanted answers.

# Chapter 18

O ne day when Cyril was on duty at the Art Gallery he met and talked to a gentleman who was admiring one of the beautiful paintings and he learned something he had not known before. It concerned Queen Victoria, and Cyril was always interested in the Queen having lived almost all his life during her reign. He admired the Queen very much. She was born at Kensington Palace in May 1819 and as a child had very little contact with children of her own age. She gave her affection to her dolls and pets and found emotional release in drawing and keeping a diary. She was only 18 years of age when she became Queen. She had never expected to succeed to the throne, but her father died two years after she was born followed by his brother George lll's death six days later. George lll's son then became George IV and when he died aged 62 in 1830 Victoria's Uncle William IV became King. He had no legitimate heir which moved Victoria up the ladder of accession. On June 19th, 1837, King William

IV died through the night and the news reached Kensington Palace in the early hours of June 20th. Victoria was now Queen of England.

Cyril thought her to be a very good Queen. She had achieved so much in her 63-year reign She had married her German cousin Albert on February 10th 1840, in the Chapel Royal, near Kensington Palace rather than Westminster Abbey, and crowds of people had gathered to catch a glimpse of her and greet her. She had twelve bridesmaids and the National Anthem was played as she processed up the aisle. After the wedding ceremony and wedding breakfast which was held at Buckingham Palace, the bride and groom drove to Windsor where they honeymooned for a week. Victoria is quoted as saying when she arrived at Windsor 'I and Albert alone – delightful'.

They had nine children: five daughters and four sons. Together Victoria and Albert set a very good example of how young children should be parented. Family life was very important to the Royal couple. They showed how much they loved their children by playing with them; reading to them; taking them on outings; and generally paying them attention and giving their time to them. In Victorian times this was not the norm because children had to grow up very quickly. They were expected to be seen but not heard, and in poorer areas children were expected to go out to work from a very young age in order to bring money in for the family income. Victoria and Albert surrounded their children with love and theirs was a very happy marriage. Victoria adored Albert and he adored her.

That is why Victoria was devastated when Albert contracted Typhoid Fever in November 1861. She and her children were at his bedside when he died on the 14th of December 1861 after only 21 years of marriage. Victoria was heartbroken and she wore black mourning clothes for the rest of her long life. She was 82 when she died in 1901, after reigning for 63 years.

The gentleman in the library was eager to tell Cyril more about Victoria. Very early in their marriage the young Victoria and her husband Albert were publicly known for their love of painting in watercolours. They were both members of 'The Water Colour Society'.

'I certainly did not know that,' Cyril said when his friend paused for breath.

'It is absolutely true,' Max continued. 'She had drawing lessons from the age of eight and was taken to many exhibitions in London as she grew up, enabling her to appreciate the works of many professional artists. She kept a journal from being thirteen years of age, writing in it almost every day, and between her marriage in 1840 and the unexpected death of Albert in 1861 she recorded hundreds of incidents of the Royal Couple looking at, commissioning and acquiring works of art of all kinds, from oil paintings to photographs, sculpture, jewellery, furniture and watercolours. They had a treasured private collection of their watercolour paintings charting the significant moments of their lives. Home and domestic life provided a common subject for Victoria's watercolour paintings.

She and Albert also painted in oils, with Albert giving Victoria lessons in technique and her painting helped her a great deal in her sorrow after Albert died. She developed a deep love for painting in nature, and Cyril's new friend Max said he was sure that one day this very Art Gallery would hold an exhibition of Albert and Victoria's paintings.

Reader, please note that in July 2019 there was a wonderful exhibition in the Laing Art Gallery of Victoria and Albert's watercolour paintings together with other wonderful watercolour paintings of their life together by various artists.

# Chapter 19

Cyril and his new friend met up in the Laing Art gallery regularly after that and it was very therapeutic for Cyril, especially when he talked about his family and the death of his son Frank. His friend was a very good listener and was especially interested in hearing about Frank because he too had worked for the railways in an administrative position before he retired.

One day Cyril asked his friend where he lived and was told he lived in Tynemouth.

'How then do you get to Newcastle?' Cyril asked.

'I come by train, of course The electric trains to the coast from Newcastle are so much faster than the previous horse drawn carriage. One day I hope to have enough money to buy a car, but until then it is the train for me. Did you know that Newcastle is the first city in the whole country to have trains run by electricity? There is so much happening in the world today, Cyril, and Newcastle is at the forefront of all the developments. We have so many entrepreneurs, inventors and outstanding engineers who have put Newcastle and the North East securely on the map. I am so proud of Newcastle. I used to live here, but when I retired my wife and I fulfilled a dream we had always had of living near the sea. Sadly, my wife did not have much time to enjoy it because she died two years after we moved. It took me a long time to overcome my grief, but I was determined not to sit around moping and doing nothing. She would have hated me doing that.

'My interest in trains has been a lifeline. I find the journeys I make to different areas in our country help me and I also come to my favourite city, this one at least once a week, which is how I met you.'

Cyril interrupted to say how glad he was that they had met. It had helped him so much to have someone different and so interesting with whom to converse and who in addition loved Newcastle as much as he did.

Max continued, 'There is always something to do or see in Newcastle and I am never bored, but I also like travelling and find it beneficial to my health. I am also very interested in photography. My camera goes everywhere with me. I have dabbled in photography for many years. Sometimes my wife got very cross with me because I can take a long time to get what, in my eyes, is the perfect picture. She also reminded me on many occasions that I always seemed to be taking other things and other people but never herself! She was right: I should have photographed her more because she was a very pretty lady. Now, as you might guess, I take numerous photographs of trains and steam engines. I have spent so many enjoyable days in the pursuit of good photographs of trains and I have learned an awful lot in the process. This does not mean that I forget my wife, but I know she would approve of what I am doing. One of these days you should come with me, Cyril, on my travels in the United Kingdom.'

'I would love to do that, Max,' Cyril replied. 'I have travelled by train to Carlisle and from there to Keswick quite a few times. Keswick is a branch line, of course, and a very scenic one, as well as being very useful for the transporting of goods to various Cumbrian towns and especially those near the sea on the fringes of Cumbria. One of my sons lives in Keswick and my wife's sister lives in Carlisle so I was very pleased that the Newcastle and Carlisle Railway was one of the first railways in the North-East to operate. It opened in 1829 and was opened in stages between 1834 and 1838. The Lake District and Carlisle is as far as I have been outside of Newcastle and I would love to visit London, our capital city. Frank, my son, was so excited when it became possible to travel by train to London, because the East Coast Mainline Train had been opened in 1850 between London and Edinburgh.'

'Why don't you come with me to London next Wednesday, Cyril? If you meet me just outside Central Station, we can get a train to London. We could stay overnight if you wish or go there and back in the same day. I really do not mind, although we will have more time to explore if we stay overnight.'

'Let us do that then. I will arrange a place to stay, if you get the rail tickets.'

Cyril told Eleanor about his trip to London, and she was excited for her father. He was recovering from the loss of his son, but this trip was just what he needed to lift his spirits even more. She helped him to pack his large bag for an overnight stay and together they walked down to the Central Station to meet up with his new friend Max. She waved him off on his adventure, having told him to be careful and look after himself. The journey was effortless, and Cyril could not believe how quickly they arrived at London King's Cross Station. After that, the day and night seemed to go so quickly and enjoyably and in no time at all they were once again boarding the East Coast Railway Carriage for the journey home. The best thing about his visit to London for Cyril had been seeing Buckingham Palace. The latter was originally called Buckingham House and was a very large townhouse built for the Duke of Buckingham in 1703 on land that had been privately owned for at least 150 years.

For more than 300 years from 1531 until 1837, the King or Queen of England's official residence in London, the capital city, was St James's Palace, located about a quarter of a mile from Buckingham Palace. St James's Palace was built by Henry VI between 1531 and 1536. He used the very best materials to build it and it is a very beautiful palace which was inhabited by Royalty until Buckingham Palace became the London residence and administrative headquarters of the King or Queen of the United Kingdom. It is the centre for state occasions and royal hospitality and is a focal point of the British people at times of National rejoicing and mourning. Queen Victoria was the first British Monarch to use Buckingham Palace and also the first to use the balcony of the building when the occasion merited it.

Cyril, being a Royalist, had always wanted to see Buckingham palace and his wish had been granted. He was very happy about that. The present king, Edward 7th, who was the eldest son of Queen Victoria, lived in Buckingham Palace. Prince Edward had waited so long to be king because his mother had reigned for 63 years and was the longest reigning British Monarch at that time. Cyril had great admiration for her. Her reign spanned a period of enormous change. Britain had the world's biggest Empire, the largest Navy, and the most modern industries. Victoria had been determined to restore dignity to the throne. She was active in state affairs and her family life with her husband Albert provided a model for the nation. When she died, she was a symbol of British Greatness and no doubt Edward would not find it easy taking her place, but he was a generous, charming, popular king and a story is told that he was devoted to his pet dog and took him everywhere. It is said that he gave his pet dog a collar with the inscription 'I belong to the King'.

Another highlight of Cyril's short stay in London was a journey on the underground railway. The Metropolitan Line had opened in London in 1863 and at first steam engines pulled the carriages which ran between roofed trenches. It was a novel experience for Cyril, and he marvelled at the engineering behind this new underground railway. He could not help thinking of Frank who would have so enjoyed hearing about his father's experience so much. He would certainly have liked a trip to London with his father, but that of course would never be possible now.

# Chapter 20

E leanor was very pleased to see Cyril smiling as he greeted his family at the Central Station. His new friend seemed just the right kind of person for Cyril and she could relax now that her father was looking and feeling so much better. Elizabeth and Jack were so glad to see their Grandpa, looking 'smiley' again and gave him loads of cuddles and kisses. It was good to be home.

Max, observing the welcome given to Cyril on his homecoming, could not help thinking what a lovely family Cyril had and when they next met in the Art Gallery, he told Cyril that he would like to take some photographs of the family. It had been a great sorrow to his wife and himself that they had never been able to have children and he was envious of Cyril's lovely family. When Cyril told Eleanor about his friend wanting to photograph the family, Eleanor thought it was a very good idea, and a few weeks later Max was invited to their home for Sunday Dinner, and to take some family photographs. Max explained during the meal that he had joined a Photography Society in Newcastle at the end of the 19th century when he was in his fifties because he was interested in the subject and his father had bought him a Kodak camera in 1888. It was easy to use because you simply pressed a button, and the camera processed the photograph for you. The slogan was 'You press the button, and we do the rest'. At the time he had thought it was magical but as he explained to Cyril, cameras had got better and better as time went on. At first all photographs were black and white, but the idea of colour photography was being explored and would certainly come one day. Max and Cyril would have been so interested to know that in the future there were great advances in photography and so many techniques developed, not least among them colour photography. They would have been pleased to know that photography is one of the biggest business successes enjoyed by millions of people throughout the world.

Max was busy all day photographing the family. Cyril, Eleanor, Tom, Elizabeth and Jack made for a lovely photograph, and Max took numerous pictures of the family in various poses. Eleanor even went to get Annabel so that she could be photographed with the family. They always thought of her as family and she had to be included. Tom and Cyril were not aware at that time or at any time how very appropriate it was to include Annabel on the photograph. On leaving that day, Max arranged to meet up with Cyril again the next week in the Art Gallery and he hoped to have the photographs processed to give to him.

Cyril usually went to Eleanor's house for tea after his visits to the Gallery and on one of those occasions she said she had something to show him. 'Father, you know how much I enjoy writing, well look what Tom has bought me, a brand-new typewriter. Gone are my frustrations of filling my pen with ink only to get unsightly blots on my paper, which I hate. I will have to learn how to use it, but it will be very useful and might even lead to a job when the children are older and more independent. I quite fancy myself as typist in an office, preferably in a school office. Typewriting is invaluable in a school office and I would love to be involved in school again. Annabel has already been to see my typewriter, Father, and says that she would like to learn to type. She could also use it for some of her schoolwork. It would be so much quicker and easier to read, she admitted, than her own writing.'

Cyril was very interested in the typewriter. He had read about the first practical typewriter being produced in 1868, followed five years later by the first commercial typewriter and very soon typewriters were used in Victorian offices to replace pen and ink. Cyril had been rather amused to learn how many women worked in offices because by 1900 most typists were women. Now his own daughter would be a typist and he was sure she would enjoy this Victorian invention.

# Chapter 21

Cyril always kept up to date with anything new and he was well aware of other inventions in the 19th century. He was fascinated by the invention of the telephone which emerged from the making and successive improvements of the electrical telegraph which was commercialised by Sir William Fothergill Cooke and came into operation on April 9th, 1839. Another electrical telegraph was independently developed and patented by Samuel Morse in 1837 and his assistant Alfred Vail developed the Morse Code signalling alphabet. America's first telegram was sent by Morse in January 1838 across two miles of wiring. It was not until 1855 that the printed telegraph was invented and it revolutionised communication. News items and other messages could be wired throughout the world, and this brought vital, quick and easy contact with other countries. When Muriel died, Eleanor and Tom were on honeymoon and it was through a telegraph that the family were able to get in touch with them and they were very grateful for that.

Many claims were made in the early days of the telephone, as to who had invented it, but two names stand out as being commercially decisive and they are Alexander Bell and Thomas Edison. The former was an inventor, scientist and innovator. He patented the first practical telephone. It is interesting that his father and grandfather had worked on a speech development programme which they called elocution, and Alexander was inspired to study communication and speech, which eventually led to his invention of the telephone. The very first telephone call occurred on March 10th, 1876. Alexander Bell and his partner Thomas Watson were in their Boston laboratory in separate rooms when Bell spoke into the mouthpiece of his new invention and said, 'Watson, come here. I want to talk to you.' At that time Mr Watson could not answer because the new telephone was only a one-way instrument, but after Thomas Edison had improved the telephone transmitter the telephone was very well used. It was the development of the telephone exchange and of a telephone number system, that transformed it into a media of communication. Few people had a telephone in their house at the beginning of the 20th century and Cyril had often wondered if Muriel would still be alive if he had been able to communicate by telephone with the hospital. He had wasted valuable time trying to communicate with the hospital. He was going to do something about installing a telephone in his home as it would be particularly helpful in an emergency. In the future it could be that his family also had telephones and it would then be much easier to keep in contact with them.

It was then that Eleanor broke into his thoughts saying, 'Father would you be able to help me with the children one afternoon in the near future? Tom and I have to attend a ceremony at the Royal Grammar School where he teaches.'

'You know the answer to that, Eleanor. I am always willing to help you with the children,' Cyril replied. 'What did you say is the occasion?'

'Remember me telling you, Father, that the Royal Grammar School moved to Jesmond in 1906? A year later, which is now of course, the opening of this new purpose-built building is being officially opened and naturally all the staff have to be present. Wives are invited so Tom and I will be going together. The 7th Duke of Northumberland is going to be there to officially open the building.'

'What date is that?' Cyril wanted to know.

'January 17th, Father, but I will remind you nearer the time. Hopefully this is the last move for the school, and I think it will be. It has moved to five different areas of Newcastle since its foundation. It began its life in a building in St Nicholas's Church graveyard, then transferred to the Virgin Mary Hospital near Westgate Road. That hospital was demolished in 1844 having been occupied by the Grammar School for nearly 250 years and the school was moved to Forth House, a very large building in the vicinity of the Central Station. Then in 1847 the school was almost extinguished because the headmaster died and because there were only twelve pupils attending, it hardly seemed worth appointing a new headmaster. The deceased headmaster's assistant, however, James Snape, was very keen for the school to continue and persuaded the council to allow him to take over. There was a lot of clearance work taking place in the area around the old Grammar School near the Central Station to make way for the new Central station to be built. The Town Councill provided the school with a new home in Charlotte Square situated near 'the Friars' in the region of Gallowgate. James Snape made a great success of the school and its numbers grew until the house became too small and inadequate, and this led to another move in 1870 to a new building in Rye Hill, once again in the West Road region of the city. That was the last move before moving to the present building in Jesmond in 1906.

'Tom loves teaching at that school, Father, and counts himself very fortunate to be teaching in a school which is the city's oldest institution of learning. We are hoping that Jack can attend that school when he is older. Tom will be able to take him with him to school, but we will have to work it all out because Tom cycles to school each day and Jack will not be able to do that if he starts at seven years of age. It is too far for a boy of his age to travel on a bicycle.'

# Chapter 22

Cyril interrupted Eleanor to remind her that in 1901 Newcastle's public transport was modernised by 'Newcastle's Corporation Tramways Electric Trams' and trams were introduced to the streets of Newcastle. It took some time to lay tramlines to the outskirts of Newcastle, but it could be that trams would be running up the West Road before Jack was due to attend school. They would just have to wait and see. Trams were certainly superior to the horses and carriages seen around Newcastle and were, of course, the forerunners of buses.

Cyril would not live long enough to see the Trolley Bus System open in 1935, which extended throughout the city until there was a fleet of 204 trolley buses covering all the Newcastle routes. The very last trolley bus to run was in October 1966. Charabancs and buses run on diesel took over after that.

'I hope Jack loves school as much as Elizabeth, Father. I have no bother with her at all. She always skips down the drive, after giving me a hug, waving goodbye and usually blowing a kiss. She really loves learning just as Tom and I do. Tom has told me the history behind his school, and it is very interesting. The school was founded in 1525 during King Henry the VIII's reign, when school master Thomas Horsley who was a Mayor of Newcastle and one of the richest merchants in the town, died, and left money in his will for the founding of the Grammar School. The first Grammar School received the Royal Foundation by Queen Elizabeth the 1st and from then on was called The Royal Grammar School, and only boys attended. Father, I would not have liked to be a pupil there in in the 16th century. The school day started at 6am and in winter the boys had to turn up with their own candle. Imagine getting up at that time in the morning to go to school and remembering to take your own candle as well as all your books for the day. It would still be dark at 6.30 in the morning which is why they had to use candles.

'We should be so thankful for electric light. It is so much easier for us now, isn't it, although I know what you are going to say, that we are all softies today and have it so easy compared to when you were growing up. As one who enjoys her creature comforts, I have to say you may be right. It is a good thing we are not all the same.'

Cyril interrupted Eleanor to say, 'No man is an island. We all need people and should always be willing to help one another, but I still wonder how there were not more fires and fatalities, especially when children handled candles. We are so fortunate to have electricity at the flick of a switch. Hurrah for the electric light bulb I say, and we are very fortunate to have been born in the Victorian Era when light bulbs were invented.'

# Chapter 23

While they were talking Annabel knocked at the door on her way home from school as she often did.

'Hi Auntie Eleanor and Grandpa Cyril. How are you both? It is so cold and dark today. I hate it when it is dark when I come out of school. We are doing a maths project at school in the form of a graph to measure how the days gradually get lighter, as winter changes to spring. You are hardly aware of it at first but little by little the day gets longer, and it is a reminder that spring is on the way. I saw another sign of spring in our school grounds today. It was in the form of green shoots peeping through the soil and I suspect they are daffodils. Grandpa, your garden is beautiful in spring with all the daffodils you have. I am looking forward to seeing them all again. They remind me of the poem that William Wordsworth wrote. Our English teacher reads us that poem every spring when the daffodils come up.'

Cyril interrupted Annabel to say, 'Benjamin has done some beautiful paintings of Wordsworth's poem about daffodils. You will have to go and visit him in the Lake District, Annabel, to see them. Your uncle is a talented artist.'

'I would love to do that someday, Grandpa, but now I want to see my little friends although they are not so little now, are they? I can hardly believe that Jack is over four and will be starting school very soon, while Elizabeth is seven and almost out of the Junior school.'

'Yes, and I am seventy now,' Cyril said. 'We are all getting older.'

Hearing Annabel's voice, Elizabeth and Jack ran into the room. They had been playing nicely together but Jack was just starting to get fractious when they heard Annabel's voice. Her presence was like magic and they settled down to play amicably. They loved Annabel and she enjoyed their company as much as they did hers, and peace reigned supreme allowing Cyril and Eleanor to continue their conversation. Something Annabel had said resonated with Cyril. She had referred to the short, long days of winter, changing very gradually as the year moved towards spring.

Cyril loved the seasons of the year each bringing its very own characteristics and they brought changes to people's way of living. Even now he was looking forward to the spring after his troubles of recent years because it brought new life to the countryside, and warmer longer days which never failed to raise his spirits. Cyril did not like the dark days of winter. They seemed to give him a sense of fear because he could not help thinking of all the people for whom there was never any light. His own grandfather had been blind, and

Cyril had never been able to come to terms with blindness. His grandfather was an example to everyone of how to cope with a severe disability, but he was very glad that he had good eyesight. Thinking about this took him back to his childhood when he used to visit with his mother an old lady called Lily.

Now as he sat drinking the nice cup of tea that Eleanor had made, using no doubt her new electric kettle, the latter having been invented in 1891, Cyril told Eleanor about the old lady he and his mother used to visit when they lived in Byker. Her house was dark as the windows were very small and when it started getting dark outside, the room was rather scary with increasingly dark shadows until this lady lit the paraffin lamp, invented in 1854, and it was her only source of light. It was a serious fire hazard if the paraffin spilt over from the lamp. The lamp was not ideal because it only gave a dim light and he used to watch the patterns it made on the walls, which was also scary. Candles were used in bedrooms, but they too were a fire hazard. My mother used to worry herself so much about Lily and her paraffin lamp and candles, but Lily said the candles gave a much better light in the bedrooms.

'Lily was so lonely and said that she dreaded the long dark nights when she just had to sit doing nothing. In the past she had had very clever hands and made beautiful fine lace but that required good light which she did not have now, and besides, her eyesight was deteriorating badly. She had never married and so had no family, and being an only child herself she had no brothers or sisters. My mother was very sorry for her and tried to help her in any way she could. We always took something home baked by my mother and

Lily was always so glad to see us. I once took her a little pot which I had made when I worked at the Maling Pottery as a young boy, and she was thrilled with it. I used to wonder many times what happened to her after we moved back to the Sandhill area of Newcastle where I was born. I hope someone else looked after her, although my grandma used to tell me that at that time when people lived in back-to-back streets or tenement buildings they did tend to help each other, so she was probably alright. There was always someone in the street to turn to in time of need. One person would be good at laying people out after death; another would be good at caring for sick children or attending to them when they hurt themselves; another could sit with a dying person; and there was always someone good at delivering babies. Your mother's mother, Eleanor, your grandma Nelly, used to be very good when helping with childbirth. She was there when you were born and helped the doctor who was grateful for her help because she was well into her labour when he reached our house and she had to get you ready for the birth. I remember it was a terrible day when I went to get the doctor. The snow was very deep, and it took a long time to bring the doctor. Your grandma's presence was invaluable.'

# Chapter 24

'Make us another cup of tea, Eleanor, because talking about light and its importance has reminded me of another great inventor of the Victorian Era and I want to tell you about him while the children are still happily occupied with Annabel.'

He and Eleanor sat down with their cup of tea and a delicious scone made by Eleanor and Cyril started to talk again. He really enjoyed airing his knowledge and sometimes he talked for too long, but she had to admit that he was very informative and interesting, and she always learnt something new from him.

'Now I have said many times, Eleanor, how fortunate we are in the North East because the North East has produced more than its fair share of inventors. Men like George and Robert Stephenson, Lord William Armstrong, Charles Parsons and Joseph Swan. He is the inventor of the light bulb which was to change the world in common with all other inventors. He was born in Sunderland in 1828 and there will be people who knew him, but I think few people fully realise what a clever man he was. He became the President of the Institute of Electrical Engineers and was knighted in 1904 for his enormous contribution to society through his services to the advancement of Electricity. He was very inquisitive as a young boy and enjoyed study and regularly visited the library in town in his teen years just as you and Tom used to do, Eleanor. He had become fascinated by the idea of electricity as a young man after hearing a lecture about it and he developed a keen interest in light and electricity, feeling sure that there was a connection between them. He had always thought it ridiculous that poorer people had to go to bed in the dark evenings of winter, when the sun set because they had no form of lighting in their houses. Joseph Swan made up his mind that he would do something about it, and he worked hard in his laboratory in the early 1840s experimenting with lighting, but it was not until 1879 that he finally mastered the intricacies of an incandescent filament lamp which led to the making of the first electric light bulb. It was such an achievement for someone who left school at 13. He obviously had a scientific bent and was good at physics and chemistry, which all played a part in his invention.

'Joseph was asked to demonstrate his achievement with a lamp bearing an electric light bulb, at the Newcastle Literary and Philosophical Society, which met in an elegant building near the Central Station. (They still meet there today.) It so happened that Lord William Armstrong was in the audience that night. You will remember, Eleanor, that your grandfather worked in one of the shipyards on the River

Tyne which was owned by Lord Armstrong. He was a great inventor himself and was very interested in the electric light bulb demonstration.

'Lord Armstrong and his wife had moved out of Newcastle to Rothbury in Northumberland in the latter years of his life and had built a very large country house there which was surrounded by big gardens and beautiful views on every side. He planted shrubs and trees to make the gardens look magnificent, the rhododendron bushes being particularly plentiful and beautiful. His house had an electrical generator driven by water from one of the many lakes on his estate. His house was already full of his own inventions such as hydraulic lifts, but he decided to use Joseph Swan's electric light bulbs to light his house. He could now use the water-power to generate electricity which would in turn allow electric bulbs to work This was why in 1880 electric light bulbs were installed in his beautiful Country Mansion at Rothbury and it became the first building in the world to be lit by hydroelectric power. The bulbs were found to be a much brighter, reliable source of light.

'It was the year after this in 1881 that street lighting using Swan's electric bulbs was put in place, although at the beginning of the 20th century most of the cities in Europe and America had streets illuminated by gas lamps. It was cheaper but not such a good light. The electric lighting was much brighter. Electricity opened up many opportunities for making homes more comfortable and life a little easier for the housewife. One of the first electrical items made for the home was the heater which converted electricity into heat, and over time there were many designs available. The electric iron was invented in 1882, followed in 1889 by the vacuum cleaner.'

Eleanor was a keen cook and remembered her mother being very pleased when gas cookers came into being in the late 19th century. In 1879 an electric oven was developed in which electrically charged wires heated a pot and by 1891 iron plates incorporated electrical elements making a much more efficient and useable electric cooker.

'You are right, Father. There are so many more things to make a housewife's work less tedious. I have always been glad that I like housework, and I do appreciate the work done by inventors. I happen to like ironing and did not mind my flat iron that I had to heat up myself on the kitchen range, but I love my new electric iron because it does a much better job and only takes half the time.

'Now, Father I am going to call Annabel and you can walk her home. I feel happier knowing that she is not walking home alone on these winter evenings, despite the street lighting.'

# Chapter 25

Cyril and Annabel walked home together and started to talk about school but there was not much time before they reached Annabel's home.

'Mum, Dad and I are going to have a serious talk tonight about my future, Grandpa, because I must give it some consideration now that I am in the first year of sixth form. I will tell you all about it when I see you next. Thank you for setting me home, Grandpa. It is like old times, isn't it?'

She waved Cyril goodbye from her front door. It was the best thing in the world to feel so loved. Her mother had a hot meal ready for her husband and daughter and they ate that before settling down to talk about Annabel's future. It was hard to believe that Annabel was 17 years of age now. She was tall, slim, and attractive with her ash-blonde curly hair and big blue eyes, and she was a clever girl. Ella and Phillip had kept all her reports from school, and they showed that her work was consistently very good and that she loved learning.

Her home life was very stable, and this showed in her good behaviour and respect for her teachers and people generally. She had a positive attitude in everything she did and was popular with her classmates. She seemed to begin and end the school day with a smile. One teacher said she was a joy to teach, which made her parents very happy and proud.

'Have you given any thought to what you would like to do when you leave school, Annabel?' her mother Ella said.

'Well, I want to do something which involves children,' Annabel replied.

'Have you thought of teaching like Auntie Eleanor, because you are very good with children?' her father said, joining in with the discussion.

'I have seriously thought about that,' Annabel said, 'but I am not sure it would suit me. I would really like to do something where I was caring for people. You see, I have seen how much Eleanor has cared for Grandpa Cyril when Uncle Frank died. He was so unhappy, and I heard him say once that he did not want to live any more. It had brought back all the memories of Muriel's tragic death. What would have happened if he had not been cared for? Then, when I was silly and tried to run away, what would have happened if you had not cared enough to come looking for me? Then I think how lucky I am that you cared so much that you chose me to adopt and be your daughter. I am the luckiest girl in the world, and I want to be in that position of caring for people. What would you say, Mother and Father, if I trained to be a nurse?'

Phillip and Ella looked at their daughter who had given them so much joy and of whom they were so proud. They assured her that she had their blessing if she wanted to train to be a nurse. She had always been a thoughtful, caring girl and a nursing career could suit her very well. Annabel said that she would talk to her teachers for advice about pursuing this career, but she also told her parents that she had been doing some reading on the subject and had found out some interesting things.

'Did you know, Mother, that nursing can be traced back to Roman times. I am full of admiration for the Romans. They were definitely a force to be reckoned with because they were intelligent, very clever people. Evidence of this can be found in so many places, not just in this country but throughout the world. There are records of the inception of nurses at the height of the Roman Empire in 300 AD. It was during this time that the Roman Empire sought to place a hospital in every single town and people assisted in in-patient medical care alongside the doctors. These people were later given the title of nurse and this remained the case for centuries. There was no formal training, and I am sorry to say, Mother, that until the mid-nineteenth century nursing was not an activity which was thought to demand either skill or training, and certainly did not command respect. Isn't that dreadful? What is more, until 1880 hospital treatment of illness was fairly rare. There were 149 hospitals in the United Kingdom in 1873 but the number has increased tremendously. There are now over four thousand hospitals and I was told only recently that I am almost sure to get a job after my training. People are recognising the true worth of nurses, especially in countries where there is warfare, and they are needed on the front line.'

'We will have to see where you can do your training,' Ella said.

'Mother, I have found out that since the 1860s many Nurses' Training Schools have opened, and someone told me that educated people were being accepted eagerly by Hospital Authorities and medical officers. Nursing is being given a much higher profile now. There is so much I will have to learn about all the advances in medicine. There are new medical techniques such as anaesthetics, new treatments and drugs for various illnesses, and there are more complicated surgery procedures. You can see, I am sure, that to gain all the new knowledge and to be able to assist doctors and medical staff training is very necessary.'

'That is certainly true,' said her father, 'but you are not afraid of hard work and are very capable of doing the studying. I think you need to talk to your teachers as soon as possible.'

'I know where I want to go, Father and that is St Thomas's Hospital in London.'

'Why that particular hospital, Annabel? It is a long way from home,' her mother said.

'My reason for choosing that hospital is its association with Florence Nightingale, whom I greatly admire. Her story fired my imagination. She opened the first Nurses' Training School in this country in 1860 and to this day it is considered one of the very best. Only the best is good enough for me, Mother. You know that,' Annabel concluded with a mischievous smile.

'I agree with you there,' her mother replied, 'but is there not anywhere nearer home. There might be a Nurses'

Training School attached to the new hospital in Newcastle, The Royal Victoria Infirmary, where James is a Doctor.'

'There will be in time, Mother, because nearly all hospitals want a Nurses' Training School on the premises or nearby, because each hospital wants to provide the very best nursing care it can, but my mind is made up. I will be 18 very soon and so in this year of 1907 I will be applying for a place at St Thomas's Hospital. I am getting quite excited talking to you about it.'

'I am getting excited for you, Annabel, and I can understand your sentiment about Florence Nightingale. She will be a great figure of history in years to come for what she did in the Crimean War. We have a great deal for which to thank her. She went out as a nurse to Crimea in 1855 to help to nurse the wounded soldiers and she was appalled and disgusted at the conditions of the British Hospital where the soldiers were treated. It was very dirty and over-run by vermin and there was a distinct lack of hygiene. She worked day and night making frequent nightly visits with her lamp so that she could see if every soldier was safely sleeping. It must have been so comforting for those soldiers knowing that someone was always there if they needed help. That was why she was known as 'The lady with the Lamp'. She was appalled by the squalid condition of the hospital and managed to train a group of nurses who cared for the wounded soldiers to the standard she required. Then Florence herself set about cleaning the entire hospital after which she made rules about handwashing and cleanliness. She is someone I admire greatly. She made people see that nursing is a very worthwhile and major profession. Indeed, she laid down the foundation of professional nursing with her high standards of cleanliness and dedication to her patients. I love her story,' Ella concluded, 'and I will be very proud if you do go to St Thomas's to do your training.'

Annabel was thrilled with her parents' response to her decision to be a nurse and the next day called in at Eleanor and Tom's to tell them all about it. They thought it was a very good choice of career, especially when Annabel told them that eventually she hoped to work on a children's ward and specialise in nursing sick children. They knew how good she was with children and how much she loved them. They had watched her playing with their children, Elizabeth and Jack, and the influence she had on them. They had always said that Annabel should choose a career in which caring for children was involved. They trusted her entirely with their children.

# Chapter 26

The day of the opening of the Royal Grammar School arrived and Cyril was ready for duty. He had not forgotten the date, despite becoming rather absent minded in his 'old age' as he called it. The ceremony was in the afternoon and Eleanor had invited him for lunch. Elizabeth was at school and he would have to meet her out of school in the afternoon. which was not a problem because he and Jack could go there together. It was a nice afternoon and while he sat in the sun Jack kicked a ball about in the garden. He could not believe it when someone shouted from the street,

'Hi, Cyril. I have not seen you for a long time. What have you been doing with yourself?'

Cyril could not believe it. It was Doris. He had hoped that she had forgotten about him. It was a long time since he had visited her house.

'You look well, Cyril, but then you always were a handsome man. How are the family? Annabel will be quite a young lady now. Do you still treat her like a daughter? I expect you do. It is strange how like Muriel she is. Did you ever find out anything at the workhouse?'

Cyril could not believe that after all this time Doris was still referring to the workhouse taunts. He decided not to answer her except to say, 'I have to go now, Doris. I am meeting my granddaughter out of school.'

He was glad to be occupied because he did not want to even think about what Doris had said. It brought back too many memories of things he did not understand. What a nasty woman she was. He was very glad that he had broken off any contact with her. As they were walking to the school to meet Elizabeth, Jack suddenly started to run, waving his arms up and down and side to side in a swooping movement.

'Jack, why are you waving your arms about like that while walking sideways?' his grandpa said.

'I am pretending to fly,' Jack replied. 'I have been listening to mummy and daddy talking about aeroplanes and I have decided that I will fly aeroplanes when I grow up. It will be so exciting. I like to watch the birds flying up to the sky and down again, and I would love to do that. It must be wonderful to be able to fly in the sky. Grandpa, do you know about aeroplanes?'

'I do know a little, Jack, but flying and aeroplanes are something quite new. I think one day it will come about that people will be able to fly up in the sky in an aeroplane but that will not be for some time. If that happens when I am still alive then you and I will definitely go up in an aeroplane together. It will be a very new form of transport and very exciting.'

'My daddy says that trains and railways were the big invention of the 19th century and aeroplanes and cars are going to be the big inventions of this century, and my daddy is always right,' Jack said confidently.

'Transport, because that is what we call it, is getting better all the time, Jack, as your father has told you. I am very interested in motor cars and I think they will come before aeroplanes. I hope to own a car one day and then you and I can go on outings in it. That will be great fun, won't it? Let's have a good talk one day about cars because I know a lot about them.'

'That will be great, Grandpa, because when I am older I want to own a car but today our legs are our transport, aren't they and we are nearly at the school. Look, there is Elizabeth,' and Jack ran towards her and gave her a hug.

# Chapter 27

On the way home Jack told Elizabeth that he and Grandpa had been talking about aeroplanes and that he was just about to tell him about the inventors of aeroplanes.

'Then I will listen too, Jack, because you know how much we learn from Grandpa.'

Cyril started his explanation. 'It was two brothers called Orville and his younger brother Wilbur and they were born and lived in America.'

'What funny names,' Jack said, chuckling.

'Jack, they were American and that is why,' Elizabeth said rather condescendingly.

'These brothers,' Cyril continued, 'were fascinated with machines and had been experimenting with engines to see if they could possibly use their engines to lift something into the air. It would be a very difficult thing to do, and they had to spend a tremendous amount of time and effort into making what would be the first Air-Plane, or aeroplane as it was later called. They must have been so thrilled when they finally succeeded in making a machine which lifted off the ground. You see, there were a lot of people fascinated with the idea of flying and there were even men who tried to fly after making various contraptions to attach to their body and arms, but all to no avail. When you are both older you can find out how those brothers eventually succeeded in making the world's first power driven machine to lift off the ground with the brothers at its controls. This was in 1903 and that very first flight was very brief, but that was only the beginning of air flight. The brothers kept on working and experimenting and I am sure that in the near future we are going to hear much more about aeroplanes becoming a popular mode of transport. It will lead up to aeroplanes carrying passengers and flying effortlessly across the skies and I also believe that aeroplanes will become so popular that they will take people to countries all over the world.'

'Grandpa Cyril,' Elizabeth said. 'Those brothers must have been very clever to invent aeroplanes and I am just thinking that aeroplanes will be the fastest way to travel. Trains are fast but aeroplanes will be faster. Am I right?'

'I am sure you are, Elizabeth, and if you work hard at school you never know what you can achieve, so keep working hard like I know you do. There, we are home again, children and I will make us some tea. Your mummy has left us some of her delicious scones for tea and there is strawberry jam to spread on them. There are also jam tarts to eat. Come and sit down because if you do not come quickly, I will eat them all myself.'

Elizabeth was always hungry when she came out of school and Jack was permanently hungry, so they hurried to the table and very soon the scones and jam tarts were all eaten. Elizabeth had helped her mummy to make the tarts the day before and they tasted so good.

It was too cold to play out of doors, but the children were content to play indoors until their mother and father returned. When they did return, Cyril could not help saying to his daughter, 'You look very smart, Eleanor. You and Tom are a very good-looking couple. Your mother and I said when you first brought Tom home that you made a handsome couple. Your mother would have been so happy to see what a lovely family you have, Eleanor. The children are a credit to you and Tom.'

'Mother always liked to see me dressed fashionably and I remember how she was always particular about the appearance of all her children. We were known for being a well-dressed family, but thank you, Father, for your compliments. We have had a lovely afternoon at the school. It was a very distinguished event with the VIIth Duke of Northumberland present and a number of other important guests. Everyone was dressed up for the occasion and fortunately it was a dry, not too cold January day. The dress that I have on, Father, I bought especially for the occasion at Fenwicks on Northumberland Street; I love that shop, one of Newcastle's first department stores. It is very up to date in fashion. When it first opened at the end of last century it was a converted doctor's house and only sold dresses and materials, but the shop is getting bigger all the time and sells all kinds of things. I love walking round such a big store especially if it is wet outside.'

Eleanor had enjoyed shopping for her special occasion dress. She was glad the ladies' fashion had moved on in 1907 from the late 1880s when dresses had a bustle at the back which she thought was very unflattering. Now, though, dresses fell smoothly over the hips and fitted snugly because they were cut on the cross. They flattered the figure which was good. Eleanor had chosen a long green dress with a fashionable high neck trimmed with lace and buttoned down the front with tiny green buttons. The long sleeves were trimmed with lace matching the high neck and the dress even had the fashionable short train at the back. Small hats were worn at the time and Eleanor's matching green lace-trimmed hat sat jauntily on her head. She was satisfied with her appearance but also bought on that shopping day in Newcastle a new skirt because she liked the new, long, bell-shape style and could not resist the fashionable lacy blouse that went with it. Cloaks or capes were often worn and three-quarter length coats were popular and she had all of those. Shoes had comparatively high heels and rounded toes and were laced up the front. Boots could be laced or buttoned and were nearly always made of leather or cloth and Eleanor wore leather buttoned boots with her green dress and long velvet gloves. She looked very attractive, and Tom was very proud to show her off that afternoon and on such a special occasion. He thought she looked as beautiful as she did on her wedding day. He also could not help thinking about the first time he saw her on the quayside that day in 1890 when she had been walking with her head bent and nearly knocked him over. He realised now that he had loved her from the moment she had lifted a tearful face up to him and so obviously needed a friend. What a lucky man he was!

Eleanor had chosen her outfit carefully because she was going to have another opportunity to get dressed up in May of 1907. Her brother Harry was going to marry Kate, his girlfriend of quite a few years, and everyone was so happy for them because Harry had taken a long time to get over Frank's death, blaming himself so much for the accident. He was much better now and marrying Kate was the best thing he could do as they were very much in love and suited one another perfectly. Harry's naval career was a great success. It was going to be a very busy year. Annabel would be having her interview for the Nurses' Training School and if successful she would start the course in January 1908 when she would be almost 18. Before that happened, she was going to be bridesmaid for Harry and Kate in the summer of 1907, and she was very excited about it.

Eleanor, Ella, Kate and Annabel had a wonderful day in Newcastle looking for wedding and bridesmaid clothes and Harry and Kate were married at St. John's Church at the bottom of Westgate Road and near the Central Station, where his friends Phillip and Ella had married in 1895. It was a rather miserable wet day, but nothing could diminish the happiness of the day for all the family, and once again Cyril was a very proud man. Harry looked extremely smart in his naval uniform. He had done so well, having qualified as a marine engineer and he was now in the Merchant Navy. The only drawback was that he had to be away from home quite frequently and Kate was worried about that until Victoria suggested to Harry and Kate that perhaps they could come and live near them in the Lake District. Victoria and Kate were already very good friends and Kate would certainly not be lonely. After due consideration this was thought to be a good solution even though it would mean extra travelling time for Harry because it was not near the coast. Harry and Kate bought a house in Keswick near to Ben and Victoria. Cyril visited his sons there as often as he could and almost always stayed with Izzy in Carlisle for a few days. Izzy enjoyed his company because she lived alone and, being a quiet, gentle sort of person, she did not socialise enough to make friends. Cyril was a very good listener and enjoyed her stories of their family as they grew up. Only two of her brothers were still alive, one of them being Archie who had done very well for himself. He was the one who had desperately wanted to read when he was very young, and Muriel had taught him with infinite patience. He was very like her in temperament too and ambitious as Muriel had once been. He had trained as a soldier and joined the army where he rose up the ranks quite quickly and earned a good salary. He now lived in London having left the army in his forties and had trained to be a solicitor. He was married, but sadly he and his wife were unable to have children and had adopted a child. He grew up to be very tall and was a guardsman at Buckingham Place. Cyril remembered how highly Muriel had spoken of her brother Archie because he could always be trusted to look after his brothers and sister Izzy, all of whom were a lot younger than Muriel. He had been particularly kind to Izzy, whenever the family had to be apart because she used to cry and cry for Muriel and her mummy. Archie had always had infinite patience with her.

Cyril enjoyed his visits to the Lake District and would like to visit more frequently which is why he was very interested in finding out about cars as a mode of transport. He had always said he would like to own a car.

# Chapter 28

L ater in the autumn of 1907 Annabel went to London to St Thomas's Hospital to be interviewed for a place at St Thomas's Nurses' Training School and there was great rejoicing when she received a letter telling her that she had been given a place there. She was to start in January 1908 and was very excited about it. One of the most exciting aspects of it for her, was the fact that she would be wearing a uniform. Annabel loved clothes. At the start of the 20th century clothes were in a much plainer style but this did not stop Annabel dressing in lace or chiffon whenever she could. She had to wear the fashionable long skirt but made sure it had lovely petticoats beneath it because when the skirt had to be pulled up to one side when crossing a road, a lacy petticoat had to be seen. Annabel liked bright colours and her favourite dress was red velvet with a very high collar trimmed with lace. One of her male admirers told her that she looked ravishing in it, which of course pleased her immensely. It would be different wearing a uniform, but she could see the reason why she had to do this, and she would be proud to wear it.

Before going to London Annabel and her mother had a shopping day in Newcastle, shopping for Christmas which would be special that year as Annabel would be nearly 18 and she was leaving home in January to begin a new life as a young adult. Annabel loved Christmas and they were going to buy a big Christmas tree this year. Annabel loved the idea of it – Queen Victoria's husband Prince Albert had introduced the Christmas Tree to England in 1840 because Christmas Trees were a big tradition in Germany. He and Victoria popularised the Christmas Tree tradition by dressing it with delicate baubles, tiny toys and shiny ribbons. Annabel loved dressing her own tree and standing it in their porch so that everyone could see it. Ella and Annabel thoroughly enjoyed their Christmas Shopping day in Newcastle especially visiting Fenwick's which was their favourite store on Northumberland Street. It had started its existence as a doctor's house until it was changed into a shop. Northumberland had once been a very pleasant street of private houses with gardens, but all the houses were eventually made into shops and business premises and it became the main thoroughfare out of Newcastle, being the road which led up from the River Tyne, through the town and out of Newcastle into Northumberland before finally reaching Scotland. Northumberland Street became famous for its shopping and was even compared as being the next best to Oxford Street in London. The two biggest stores on the street were Fenwick's and Marks and Spencer's.

Christmas 1907 was a very happy occasion for the whole family. Cyril, Eleanor, Tom, Elizabeth, Jack, Ella, Phillip and Annabel were joined by Benjamin, Victoria and Edward. Victoria was now pregnant with their second baby and they were hoping for a second son. The newly-weds, Harry and Kate, were also there, and the family were delighted to learn that Kate was expecting their first child. Seeing almost all his family together meant so much to Cyril, even though Muriel and Frank were missing but they would never be forgotten.

In January 1908 the family said a rather emotional goodbye to Annabel when she left to go to London to begin her nursing training. She looked upon it as an adventure but knew that she would miss her family terribly. Growing up was not always easy but she had to face the future and wanted to be successful in her chosen career. Elizabeth cried and cried as she waved goodbye to her best friend, but Annabel promised that she would be back to see her and told her that she must keep on working hard at school and then she would be successful in what she chose to do in her life. She also asked Elizabeth to look after Grandpa and make sure he was happy. Jack was very sad to see her go but she told him to learn as much as he could about aeroplanes so that he could tell her all about them when she came home, because they would definitely be an exciting mode of transport in the future, and he might even grow up to be a pilot himself. Jack wanted to go to the library immediately to read some books about aeroplanes until his father said it was too early for books to have been written about flying and aircrafts. Tom promised his son that as soon as books were written he would take him to the library to find out more.

Eleanor really missed Annabel, and in an attempt to cheer her up Tom told her one day when she and Tom returned from school that he had bought her a special present and he took her on her own into the Drawing Room. When she unwrapped the parcel Eleanor could not believe her eyes. It was a vacuum cleaner. She usually brushed her carpets by hand but then a type of vacuum cleaner had been invented. The earliest model made in 1889 was not too effective because it blew dust away from the vacuum rather than sucking it up. Eleanor did not use it very often because it was harder work to do so. The dust which blew around had to be swept up by a hand brush. She had heard some years ago, 1901 she thought it was, that a new successful suction vacuum had been invented. She had thought it would be a good idea to buy one of those but had never talked it over with Tom, and yet here he was buying her the very thing she wanted. She was delighted and gave Tom a big hug. She thanked him profusely saying:

'Tom, thank you. It is just what I have wanted for some time and will be such a help with my housework. I am really doing well because I have an electric iron too, as you know. It is not ideal but still better than the flat iron which had to be put on the fire to heat. As you know I have a cooking range in my kitchen which makes heating a flat iron easier, but I am thrilled to have an electric iron. How cleverly made it is. I am glad the electric iron has been invented.

'When did you say it was invented, Tom?' Eleanor wanted to know.

'The cordless electric iron was invented in 1882 and the heat came from an electric element in its stand,' Tom told her.

'I love it,' Eleanor said, 'and it will really help me with my housework. In fact, all the inventions are really helping ladies to keep their houses clean.'

Annabel had packed her 'ravishing' red dress just in case there was an occasion to wear it. She secretly hoped that she could meet someone tall, dark and handsome who would take her out to dine in an expensive restaurant and then she could wear the beautiful red dress. She had settled down very well in London to everyone's relief and was thoroughly enjoying her nurses' training. She had also made many friends and was very happy. Elizabeth wrote little letters to her best friend Annabel in her best writing, while Jack drew or painted pictures for her to include in the envelope. Annabel was delighted with them.

She missed her family terribly but there was plenty of work to do and she worked hard. One day she wrote to say that she had been asked out by a gorgeous young man for an evening meal at a 'posh' hotel and she was going to wear her 'ravishing red dress'. After the event she wrote to say that she was sure she was falling in love with the gorgeous young man. Annabel 'fell in love' quite a few times while in London but just before she completed her second year at the Nursing School, she said she was very much in love with a very tall handsome man who was a guardsman at Buckingham Palace. She wanted to bring him home so that her parents could meet him. She was sure she had found her true love. He had told her that he had connections with Northern England and would be telling her parents all about it.

# Chapter 29

After Annabel left for college, Cyril had pursued in earnest his idea of buying a car. He knew that only the rich could afford to buy a car at the beginning of the 20th century, but Cyril very much wanted to buy a car. Interest in the making of cars as a means of transport had begun in the middle of the 19th century, when in 1885, a man called Karl Benz built a gasoline engine and fixed it to a three wheeled carriage and made the world's first practical, gas powered car in 1885. It ran on flat land only and did not have enough power to go up hills. It had to be pushed uphill and consequently no-one was interested in such a vehicle, and so Karl Benz had to keep working on his original model. He added gears which helped the model to go up hills and was soon developing successful four-wheeled cars, until by the beginning of the 20th century he was the world's leading car maker. Cyril had followed this man's progress with interest and wondered if anyone else would take up the challenge of this new form of transport. It was not long before Benz had competition in two men, called Gottlieb Daimler and William Maybech whose joint efforts had produced the first motorbike, but by 1889 they were building cars and ten years later formed the Daimler Company. Their cars were very expensive and only the very rich could buy them, but Cyril hung onto the hope that one day they would be cheaper to buy. A car would give him the opportunity to travel further afield, and it would be much easier to visit his sons and grandchildren in the Lake District. He might even be able to visit Annabel in London, although the train was definitely the fastest way to get there.

The horse remained the most reliable source of road transport, pulling along as it did bus styled carriages and other vehicles. It was not until an American engineer saw the horse as a challenge that things changed. This American was born in 1863 and was called Henry Ford. He had been interested in engines from being a young boy, and loved and understood machinery. He was determined to create an engine which could become a replacement for horse-power. He first built a little car which looked little more than a four wheeled motorbike and was called a Quadricycle. Then he decided to make the simplest possible horseless carriage and he would make it in such quantities and only in one colour, so that it could be sold cheaply to a huge number of people. It took him 12 years to get it right and he made eight different models, calling them by alphabetical letters: A, B, C, F, N, R, S and K before finally coming up with a winner, the Model T. This car was launched in 1908 and was a car everyone could afford. Around 15 million Model T Fords were eventually sold and a delighted and very rich Henry Ford felt he had at last given people a much more comfortable, better and faster mode of travel as opposed to a vehicle pulled by a horse. In his eyes a car was easier to maintain than a horse which needed feeding and stabling and took up much more of a person's time. Henry Ford will always be a hero for putting cars within the reach of ordinary people.

It was such good news for Cyril that a car made by Henry Ford was made available in 1908 at a price he could afford, and he decided to buy one. He was the only person in Summerhill to own a car and it stood proudly outside his house. All the family came to inspect it and soon Cyril was very busy taking his family out for drives and generally showing off his new form of transport. When Annabel came home on the train from London, as she did quite often, Cyril was proud to pick her up from the Central Station and Annabel thought it splendid that she could be picked up in style. Almost every weekend Cyril took Eleanor, Tom, Elizabeth and Jack and their good friends Phillip and Ella down to the coast and either rode or walked along the road from Tynemouth to Whitley Bay, or spent the day playing on the sand with the children. They were very happy days, memories of which would comfort the family in years to come. Cyril felt it was a great asset to the family and was giving so much pleasure. He was thrilled with his new Ford car but was not yet confident enough to travel a long distance in it until Ben and Harry asked him to come for a holiday in Keswick. There was a special reason for this. Ben and Victoria now had a second son whom he had not met, and a baby girl had just been born to Harry and Kate which was why Harry was home on leave. His sons were very keen to see Cyril's car and so it was decided that he would spend Easter with them, and so with a sense of trepidation Cyril set off in his Model T Ford Car to travel to Keswick. He had been going to stay overnight in Carlisle with Muriel's sister Izzy but had changed his mind and was going there on his way home. The last time he had seen her was when Frank had had the accident, and so he was looking forward to visiting her. He vaguely remembered that she had made some strange remarks the last time he saw her, but that did not bother him yet.

His first long car journey to Keswick was uneventful and when he arrived at the home of Ben and Victoria, Edward ran out to welcome him. Victoria stood at the door with their new baby son George in her arms. Springtime in the Lakes is a lovely time of year when everything is coming to life again and Cyril had a great time with the boys as they pointed out the new lambs in the field and stood beside the lake throwing pebbles to make ripples on the water. In the park they kicked their ball around and even went looking for frogspawn in the many streams found in the countryside around Keswick. It was a magical time which Cyril would never forget. All too soon it was time to set off for home with a stop in Carlisle to see Izzy, but the visit was to be very different from what he imagined.

# Chapter 30

Izzy welcomed him warmly after admiring his new car.

'My neighbours will be very curious, Cyril. You will not see any cars around here. No one could afford one. Now sit down and I will make us a cup of tea and we can catch up with all our news. Last time we had no time to talk if you remember because we had to make an emergency dash to Carlisle hospital. I was so sorry about Frank's death. What a shock for you all.'

'It was certainly a terrible time, Izzy and without my family I could never have got through it,' Cyril said. 'Eleanor, my daughter, has been absolutely wonderful in looking after me.'

'I am not surprised, Cyril. Girls are definitely the best when it comes to looking after their fathers and I expect your other little girl was a good help too. What did you say you had called her?'

'Izzy, I do not have any other daughters. I remember you asking me that last time I saw you and I was very puzzled.'

'Muriel did not have a name for the baby when she left here after the baby was born,' Izzy said.

'Izzy, I know nothing of a baby. I only have one daughter called Eleanor. Tell me again about this other baby which you say belongs to Muriel.'

'Cyril, l delivered your second daughter in this house because I am a qualified midwife. You must remember Muriel coming here to have her baby, even though it is some time ago now. It must be eighteen years ago. My daughter was here at the time so she would be able to verify what I have said. I must say that at the time I wondered why you were not with Muriel.'

Cyril was feeling very discomfited.

'The reason I was not with her, Izzy, is because I did not know that she was having another baby. I still cannot believe what you are telling me because Muriel would not do something like that. I trusted her entirely for all our years of marriage and I definitely know that she was faithful to me, and so your story just is not possible.'

Izzy was beginning to feel very embarrassed. It was obvious that Cyril knew nothing about the baby she had delivered, and she hesitated to say any more, but Cyril was determined to get to the truth.

'Izzy, did Muriel leave your house very early in the morning?'

'Definitely, Cyril, because my daughter's husband needed to be in Newcastle early that morning and he said he would give Muriel and her baby a lift home to Newcastle.'

ELEANOR'S SECRET REVEALED

An increasingly worried Cyril said, 'I remember the morning when she arrived home very early, but she had no baby with her.'

'She must have had, Cyril. She could not wait to get back to you after she had the baby and that is why she accepted a lift from my son-in-law who very conveniently had a meeting in Newcastle that morning. I told her it was too cold to take such a tiny baby out so early in the morning, but she wrapped her in a beautiful shawl which she had knitted herself, and which she said had served all her other five children and was adamant that she had to get back to you. Ted, my son-in-law, told me that he dropped Muriel and the baby off at the Workhouse on Westgate Road. He wanted to take her to your house, but she insisted that she had to get off at the Workhouse. It was an easy walk home from there as it was downhill all the way. Strange, really, when she could have been taken right to the door especially with a baby in her arms.'

# Chapter 31

C yril felt quite faint. Izzy was obviously telling the truth, but he could not believe what she was telling him. The word Workhouse went round and round in his head. Could Muriel possibly have been the lady who abandoned the baby at the Workhouse before she came home that morning? It was a tremendous shock for him. He had to have time to think. He had so many questions to ask.

Izzy could see how upset Cyril was and left him alone while she went to prepare a meal for them. Something was desperately wrong. Why had Muriel not told Cyril about the baby? That was a shocking thing to do and more importantly where was the baby now? Cyril was distraught and he did not deserve that. She had always liked him and rather envied her sister Muriel for having such a caring husband. She could feel tears pricking the back of her eyes because her innocent words had obviously revealed a family secret.

As Cyril sat thinking, a number of things began to fall into place. Muriel had not talked at all about her trip to Carlisle to see her sister when she returned so early that morning. He had just thought she was tired after the journey. His thoughts went back to that time when he had read out that article in the newspaper about a baby being abandoned on the door of the Workhouse. It could not have been Muriel because she had straightaway commented that there must be something the matter with someone who could do such a thing. She would not have said that if she had been the one to leave the baby. Izzy must be mistaken. Muriel did not have a baby and yet she had seemed to be telling the truth. It was all very confusing. Surely, he would have known if Muriel was pregnant. How could he not! She would have told him he was sure of that and any baby she had would definitely be his. Muriel would never have been able to hide an affair from him because they did everything together. She had no reason whatsoever to hide a pregnancy from him and the idea of a baby belonging to him being abandoned on a doorstep did not bear thinking about. In fact, he could feel sobs rising in his throat at the very thought of it. He sat for a long time staring at the fire crackling in the hearth. Somehow the crackling of the fire and the warmth of the room comforted him.

Izzy eventually brought in the meal and Cyril ate it in silence and for the rest of the evening he made no conversation with Izzy and was glad when it was time for bed, although once in bed he could not sleep. Thoughts of Muriel went round and round in his head. How could Muriel possibly have had a baby he did not know about? It could not be true. There had to be another explanation. It could have been a bundle of clothes that the woman was leaving on the step, and the woman could have been anyone and he convinced himself that that was the explanation.

If Muriel had found herself pregnant, she would have told him. There was no shame attached to a baby conceived within marriage even if the parents were older. Doris's words came back to him 'Would you have liked a second daughter, Cyril?' She must have known something about Muriel and a baby that he did not. It was she who had so cruelly mocked Annabel and called her the Workhouse girl. Now it was making some sense. The word Workhouse was the key and Doris must have seen someone leaving the baby when she had worked there some time ago. It was all coming together now. Doris must have seen Muriel leave the baby on the doorstep of the workhouse, which is why she was asking him all those questions and hinting all the time that he was the baby's father.

Then he sat up in bed with a jolt as his mind took him back to Eleanor's wedding when Annabel was bridesmaid. It was when the bride and bridesmaids were walking up the aisle and reached the front of the church that Muriel had gasped and sat down abruptly. Her face was white, and she had begun shaking. He had asked her if she was unwell, but she said she was fine. He knew for the rest of the ceremony that she was far from well, but she had said nothing more about it and she had died the next day without explaining what had made her unwell in church. Then he remembered that when he saw Annabel in the bridal procession, he had noticed certain similarities with his wife. It was rather uncanny just how like Muriel she was with her ash blonde, very curly hair and big blue eyes, and he remembered Eleanor saying that Ella and Phillip's little girl Annabel had a beautiful singing voice just like Eleanor's mother. Was it at all possible that Annabel was related to them? There had been so many veiled references to Muriel and another baby. Cyril felt very confused, but could it possibly be that Muriel, who had never met Annabel before, had looked at her and realised that she could be the child she had abandoned? He could relate this idea to things that had been said to him by Doris and by Izzy, Muriel's sister. If all this was true, then he had been very naïve. Surely, he would have sensed that Annabel was his very own child. They had become very close, and he loved her as if she was his own but never had it crossed his mind that she was actually his own child. He had trusted Muriel completely and to his knowledge they had always been honest with one another throughout their married life. There had never been secrets between them. He just could not believe that Muriel had deceived him. Something was very wrong. Looking back, he should have asked more about Muriel's trip to see her sister in Carlisle and asked why she had come home so soon and so early one morning all those years ago. If he had done so Muriel could be alive today because as he realised now Muriel had had a tremendous shock when she saw Annabel and the shock could have led to the horrific, fatal asthma attack she had suffered. He must get home and talk to Eleanor because there were questions he needed to ask and to which he wanted answers.

# Chapter 32

The next morning Cyril was up early. He would have liked to stay longer with Izzy who said she had been very lonely since her husband had died, but he had to see Eleanor and find out if she knew anything at all about her mother's deceit. Things had to be sorted out one way or another.

Izzy tried to get him to stay but he was adamant that he had to get home.

'I am so sorry, Cyril, that I have upset you so much. I just did not know the truth about Muriel's baby. She swore me to secrecy about the reason why she had come to see me because she had to sort things out with you. I never thought for a moment that she was not going to keep the baby. How could she possibly have left that beautiful baby on a doorstep? There is no excuse for that, however desperate she felt. I do know, Cyril, that it was your baby because one of the things she said was that you had both decided that you did not want any more children because you, Cyril, were not good with small babies and all the attention they need. She kept saying how much she loved you and that your relationship would have suffered if she had another baby. I think too that she felt she was too old to have a new baby and would feel embarrassed about the eighteen-year age gap, between Eleanor and the baby. She also said that she had been enjoying time for herself after bringing up a family of five and that she loved the freedom of doing what she wanted to do and when she wanted to do it. It sounds very selfish put like that, but I do not think she had thought it through enough. She just wanted life to go on as it had before she became pregnant. You must believe me, Cyril, when I tell you that she kept saying how much she loved you.'

Cyril was listening carefully and said, 'Izzy, she should have given me the chance of knowing about the baby and I am sure that together we could have worked it out. I keep wondering how I did not notice that she was pregnant. It certainly was not too obvious, and I remember her once saying that she and her friends were always moaning about the fact that they were developing a middle age spread so I thought no more of it. How could she deceive me in that way? I am hurting, Izzy. I am hurting very much but I have been very stupid.'

'No, Cyril,' Izzy said, putting her arm around him. She felt so sorry for him. He was still grieving for his wife and son, and now he had the added burden of Muriel's betrayal.

'You are certainly not stupid, Cyril,' Izzy told him. 'You are a lovely man who never sees any wrong in anybody and I know how much you adored Muriel. You do not deserve being treated like that. No blame can be attached to you. I am horrified at what my sister has done, but she has paid a heavy price for her wrong-doing.'

'What do you mean by that, Izzy?' Cyril said.

Izzy's answer confirmed what he had been thinking through the night.

'I think, Cyril, there is a connection between Muriel's deceit and her sudden death. I might be wrong, but you must have a really good talk with Eleanor when you get home and together you may come up with an answer. Now I am going to make you another cup of tea and then you can set off for home, but you must drive carefully, because you are still so upset. We do not want any more accidents.'

Cyril could not help thinking that Izzy was a lovely, caring person.

# Chapter 33

C yril did drive carefully but could not forget what had
happened. He kept remembering different things which
were making it more and more clear that it was Muriel who
had been seen at the workhouse and it was his baby that
she had left there. Then he remembered something which he
had heard when he visited the workhouse. Someone at the
workhouse had said that the baby was wrapped up securely
in a beautiful hand knitted shawl. Muriel had knotted a
beautiful shawl when she was expecting their first baby and
she had used it for all their subsequent babies. It could be a
coincidence, but it was beginning to look very unlikely. Cyril
felt sick to even think that Muriel, the wife he had adored,
had managed to deceive him very successfully. His image
of her now was tarnished. She had never owned up to the
police when they asked for information and had actually
committed a criminal offence. She had managed to avoid
blame by being very underhand and secretive. How had

she dared to tell so many lies and shame her family? He felt disgusted and angry at the same time because she had succeeded in deceiving him massively. How was he going to tell his family because they really needed to be told?

When he reached home from the Lake District that day he went straight out to Eleanor's house and she immediately knew something was amiss. Her father's face looked haggard as if he had been crying and his words were slightly incoherent at first.

'Eleanor, I have had such a shock while I have been away and we must sit down and talk about it. I have heard something unbelievable about your mother and have some questions I would like to ask you.'

Eleanor knew instinctively that this was going to be the moment of truth and her secret was going to be told.

'Did you know, Eleanor, that your mother had had another baby?'

'Yes I did, Father,' she answered truthfully, 'but I could not tell you.'

'Why could you not tell me, Eleanor?'

'Father, Mother needed to be the one to tell you and I waited and waited for her to do so but she never did, and I have had to keep the secret for almost eighteen years. I have hated myself for doing so, but if I had told the family it would have torn us all apart.'

'Tell me, Eleanor, truthfully. Is Annabel my daughter?' Cyril asked with a tremble in his voice.

'Yes, she is, Father,' Eleanor said fearfully because she could see the strain on his face, 'but no-one else knows, Father. I have kept that secret for a long time.'

'These revelations are too much for me, Eleanor,' Cyril said, collapsing into a chair. 'What am I to do? Everything is such a mess.'

Eleanor was worried about her father. She had been afraid of this day for a very long time. She knew her father would be devastated to learn that his wife had deceived him in such a dreadful way and that he had actually fathered another child. She had suffered heartache knowing about her mother's deceit, but it would be so much harder for her father. From that day she felt that he was a changed man. He always appeared to have something on his mind and the endless patience which he had always had with her children, Elizabeth and Jack, was no longer there. She was glad that Annabel was away in London because at least Cyril did not have the same contact with her, and he had time to come to terms with the fact that she was his daughter. He would have to work out how he was going to manage the situation without hurting too many people, least of all Phillip and Ella whom she knew as her parents. He could not hurt them. He had a lot of thinking to do.

Eleanor felt a great burden had been lifted from her shoulders now that her father knew about the baby, but they had to decide if the family should be told. Meanwhile she was relieved when her father took up his walking hobby again. He used to take his car out into the countryside, leave it somewhere and walk considerable distances away from it before returning to it and going home. He found solace in the countryside. There was a peace there which helped to heal the hurt, anger and resentment within him. In time he felt able to face the world again and even think of the future.

Sometimes he took his car to Tynemouth, parked it and then went for a long walk. One of his favourite places to walk was along the top of the cliffs at Whitley Bay, which led him to St Mary's Lighthouse. If the tide was out, he could walk across the little causeway to the island and find a large stone on which he could sit and stare out to sea. It was as if his hateful thoughts and feelings of resentment could be cast onto the waves which the ebbing tide would take out to sea and he had a sense that he was being healed. Over time Cyril was healed and felt able to carry on with his life. He could forgive Muriel whom he had loved for so many years. She had been such a loving wife and mother and they had meant so much to one another. Sadly, she had made one very big, fatal mistake. He had always had an affinity with Annabel and would carry on just as he always had with her. No good could come of him telling her he was her father, but he could rejoice as a father would, at all her achievements. He could also rejoice at all the things about her that reminded him of Muriel. He felt that she was a gift from Muriel and that was the way he was going to look at it. He was sure that Muriel must have regretted what she did and must have been heartbroken at abandoning her own baby. He was going to look forward and be brave because his lovely daughter Eleanor had been very brave to keep her secret for so long, he had to be strong for her. He would now take on the secret and no-one else need ever know. In her sons' eyes she would remain the loving mother that they knew and who had loved them all so dearly. It would remain a mystery for ever as to why she did what she did. He called in at Eleanor's on his way home after one of his trips to St Mary's Island and looked so invigorated that

Eleanor said he looked like his old self again. He told her that she could confide in him about anything and everything, and especially if there was any more trouble in the family. Eleanor promised she would do that and there were to be no more secrets.

One afternoon not long after he and Eleanor had spoken to one another about Muriel's baby, Cyril decided to go on his walk up the West Road and back down a side street. He had not noticed that this was the street where Doris lived and as he walked past it a familiar voice shouted from a window.

'Cyril, it is great to see you again after all this time. How are you? I see you are as handsome as ever. What about your family? You must tell me, so come inside and have a cup of tea.'

Once inside Doris began her interrogation but not before Cyril had noticed that the room was more richly furnished than before, and Doris herself was dressed much more smartly. Something must have changed since he last saw her.

'What do you think of my house now, Cyril? It has changed since I last met you. I am married now to my second husband who has a very good job and I am much better off financially.'

'Where are your children now'? Cyril asked.

'I never see them,' Doris answered. 'They live their own lives and I do not want to be part of them. Both my sons have been in prison for minor offences and my daughter has three children under four years of age, all with different fathers. I blame their father for everything that has happened to them and just leave them to it.'

'Doris, that is a very harsh way to talk about your own children. You must have some feelings for them,' Cyril said incredulously.

'None at all, Cyril. Sidney and I are as happy as can be and I will not let anything interfere with that,' Doris replied rather huffily.

She continued, 'Did you ever find out if that pretty little girl called Annabel belonged to you, Cyril, because she was your baby. I knew that. Fancy your own wife not telling you she was pregnant with your baby. What a disgrace. Muriel really let you down, didn't she? No breeding obviously.'

Doris was so enjoying watching Cyril's face as she lashed out at him that she hardly noticed the door close as he left her house in utter disgust. What a terrible woman she was. He never wanted to see her again, but his thoughts turned to one woman whom he did want to see again. She was the complete opposite of Doris. She was kind, gentle, thoughtful, caring and understanding; in fact, as nice a person as her sister Muriel, his late wife.

# Chapter 34

E leanor had some news for Cyril when he went to her house after his encounter with Doris.

'Father, you will never guess, but Annabel is getting engaged to the handsome Guardsman she told us about, but that is not all. Adam, the man she is to marry, is the adopted son of Archie, Mother's brother. What do you think of that?'

'Wonderful news and there might be more happy news soon, but I am not going to tell you yet. I will tell you, however, that I am going to Carlisle tomorrow to see Izzy.'

'Why are you going to Carlisle, Father? We agreed that there were to be no more secrets.'

'I want to see Izzy, Eleanor. I have enjoyed her company when I have seen her in the last two years and today, I suddenly realised that I would like her in my life permanently. So much has happened in our family and she has helped me a great deal by listening and understanding how I felt. I need to see if she feels the same way about me as I do about her.'

Eleanor could not have been more pleased. This would be the beginning of a new life for Cyril. Izzy was a lovely person and very lonely since her husband had died and her daughter had emigrated to Australia.

So it was that Cyril, a few days later set off in his car to go to Carlisle. When Izzy opened the door, she was surprised to see Cyril standing there.

'What a lovely surprise,' she said. 'Come along inside while I make us a cup of tea.'

When they sat down Izzy asked Cyril why he had come to Carlisle.

'I have come, Izzy, to thank you for being so understanding and kind when I was desperately worried, and even frightened for my future. I have come to realise that you mean a great deal to me and I want to show you how much I care about you.'

'Cyril, you are making me blush. I care about you so much and I felt so miserable when you went home the last time because I knew you were very upset. Can you stay for a few days and we can talk and get to know one another better?'

'That is a really good idea, Izzy. We can also have some outings in my car and of course we must visit Ben and Victoria and Kate. Harry is away at sea so he will not be there but you have not seen Ben and Victoria's new baby son George, so they will be very pleased to see you.'

There followed a week of the happiest days Cyril had spent for a long time and one evening when they were standing at one of their favourite places, namely Friars Crag, Cyril asked Izzy to marry him. She had no hesitation in saying yes.

She returned to Newcastle with Cyril and they lost no time in making arrangements for their wedding in St Matthew's Church in Summerhill where they were to live. Cyril could not see any point in waiting to be married. They needed one another now. Annabel was going to be a special guest

at the wedding because she was going to sing with her now trained, beautiful singing voice. Elizabeth, who was ten years old now in 1910, would be a bridesmaid and Jack now eight years of age would stand together beside Cyril and Izzy. Jack asked if he could wear his Royal Grammar School uniform for the wedding. It was brand new because very soon he would be starting school there. Tom said it was a great idea and on the Wedding Day Elizabeth and Jack were in front of the procession with their parents and uncles and aunties, joining Cyril and Izzy at the front of the church. It was such a happy occasion because once again the family were all together and as always Muriel and Frank were in everyone's thoughts.

Before the wedding took place Cyril wanted to celebrate his engagement to Izzy and he decided to take Izzy out for a very special meal in Newcastle. Eleanor, Tom, Elizabeth and Jack, together with Phillip and Ella and Tom's parents were joining them and also Max, Cyril's friend from the Gallery. Cyril had chosen a restaurant housed in a beautiful architectural building called 'The Emerson Chambers'. It stood on the site of a former Presbyterian church on Blackett Street within sight of Grey's Monument and was built in 1903. The building is unique, because of its highly decorative baroque style, with elaborate copper domed towers and even some oriental ornamentation. At the top of the building, a little difficult to see, there is a copper-clad two-faced clock. The building was designed for a restaurant in the basement and three other floors to house shops and offices. It is a very tall building and when it was built a beautiful staircase led down to the basement from the street giving it a sense of grandeur. It was the perfect setting for a celebration meal. Cyril could not know then that in the 21st century this very tall grand building is completely used by Waterstones Book Store. It is fitting for Cyril's family that books are a major feature in the use of the building.

The family had a splendid evening there and there was a special surprise not long after they had started eating. Two very attractive people came through the door. The young man was very tall and handsome, and the young girl was dressed in a 'ravishing' red dress. Reader, you do not need me to tell you who they were, and you can imagine, I am sure, what delight the visit brought the family. At last Cyril was looking at Annabel as his daughter, his sixth child, and he was so proud. She was a beautiful, caring, loving girl who had brought so much happiness into the lives of Cyril and his family and of course her adopted parents Phillip and Ella.

There were actually two engagements to celebrate that evening because Adam and Annabel had just got engaged, too. Max had brought his camera and he took a great many photographs, especially of the Lady in Red, who had made the dramatic entrance with her Guardsman fiancé. Cyril once again looked round proudly at his family while also remembering Muriel and Frank who would always be part of it.

After such a wonderful evening it was time to make the final arrangements for the wedding of Cyril and Izzy. They were going to live in Cyril's house in Summerhill and when Izzy's house was sold in Carlisle, they were going to buy a cottage in the Lake District which they both loved. They would be able to see more of Harry, Kate and their new baby girl Annie and more of Benjamin and Victoria and their sons Edward and George. Eleanor, Tom and their children would be able to stay with them whenever they wanted to and James would always be a welcome visitor.

The wedding of Cyril and Izzy took place at St. Matthew's church on a sunny day in June 1910. It was a beautiful service and Annabel sang a beautiful Aria in the middle of the service, which delighted everyone. There was another member of the congregation who liked to be heard and who only out of curiosity wanted to be part of the wedding. After all, in her mind she might have been the groom's wife if things had worked out differently. Cyril had been her very first love. Reader, I am glad to say the Doris behaved herself in church that day.

Their guests included, of course, Annabel and her handsome guardsman fiancé Adam, in full Guardsman's uniform. Annabel had qualified as a nurse and was working in the hospital where she had trained. She was still singing with her beautiful voice and sang at her 'father''s wedding to everyone's delight and admiration.

It was a very special wedding and so we leave Cyril and Izzy as they begin their married life and wish them and all their family every happiness in the future.

A second wedding did take place exactly a year after Cyril and Izzy got married. The bride looked absolutely beautiful and with Adam her future husband in full guardsman's uniform they made a stunning couple. Hidden somewhere on Annabel's wedding dress was pinned a small brooch which said, 'State Registered Nurse'. She was so proud of that brooch. Cyril's heart nearly exploded with pride when he looked at his beautiful daughter. He was now the holder of the secret which Eleanor had kept for so long, and it would remain a secret forever but now he could acknowledge his daughter in his heart without anyone else knowing the truth and he was content. You could say truthfully that Cyril and his family lived happily ever after, or as Shakespeare would have said, 'All's well that ends well'.

*The End*

www.ingramcontent.com/pod-product-compliance
Lightning Source LLC
Chambersburg PA
CBHW060929120626
46557CB00003B/932